ALL
YOURS,
STRANGER

Also by the same author

Marry Me, Stranger
Ex
How About a Sin Tonight?
That Kiss in the Rain
A Thing beyond Forever

NOVONEEL CHAKRABORTY

ALL YOURS, STRANGER

EBURY
PRESS

An imprint of Penguin Random House

EBURY PRESS

USA | Canada | UK | Ireland | Australia
New Zealand | India | South Africa | China

Ebury Press is part of the Penguin Random House group of companies
whose addresses can be found at global.penguinrandomhouse.com

Published by Penguin Random House India Pvt. Ltd
7th Floor, Infinity Tower C, DLF Cyber City,
Gurgaon 122 002, Haryana, India

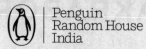

Penguin
Random House
India

First published by Random House India 2015

Copyright © Novoneel Chakraborty 2015

21

ISBN 9788184006858

Typeset in Requiem Text by Manipal Digital Systems, Manipal
Printed at Replika Press Pvt. Ltd, India

www.penguin.co.in

MIX
Paper from
responsible sources
FSC® C016779

For my father . . .

Thanks for that Howard Roark gene. I shall be forever indebted to you for this and a lot more.

Prologue

The photograph of love is sometimes so big that you can't fit it into the frame of your relationship. If you force it, you are sure to lose some of it. Maybe most of it.

Sitting at the bar, Rivanah watched as her boyfriend Danny danced with the 'other' girl in a close embrace. Rivanah had promised herself she wouldn't drink since the next day was Monday and Monday-morning hangovers made her feel the world was conspiring to bring her down. Minutes back the three of them had been sitting on a couch. It was when Rivanah had stood up to get her Virgin Mojito refilled that the 'other' girl Nitya had asked, 'May I ask your boyfriend for a dance?' Rivanah had given her a tight smile of acknowledgement.

Nitya was one of those people you could never be 'friends' with and there was no reason why. But Rivanah couldn't afford to be indifferent to her because Nitya was her boyfriend's best friend. On other days, Rivanah neither liked nor disliked Nitya but she hated her whenever she started a statement with 'May I ask your boyfriend for . . . ?' Why this seeking of permission? To Rivanah, it always sounded as if the statement was gravid with a hidden taunt for her to decipher. As if Nitya would have left Danny alone had Rivanah said no. As if Danny too would have said no to Nitya if Rivanah had said no. Rivanah would have skipped accompanying them to the nightclub but today was Nitya's birthday and Danny had requested Rivanah to join them. As usual she couldn't say no to Danny and now she was sitting at the bar, like a loser, watching her boyfriend and his best friend groove to the latest chartbuster.

'Absolut,' Rivanah said to the bartender instead of asking for a refill of her Virgin Mojito. The bartender was quick to serve her and she was quicker to gulp it. She noticed Danny flash a smile at her (did he?) and then his face was turned the other way by his best friend. *Have they slept behind her back?* Rivanah was ashamed of asking herself this question but it was not the first time she was doing so. There were questions she could never answer. Questions about loyalty, trust and infidelity in a relationship. If love was really no contract then how does cheating come into being? Or was love an unsaid emotional contract after all? She gulped three more shots of Absolut and ordered the fourth, turning her face spitefully away from the 'best friends'.

'You remind me of someone.'

Rivanah turned her head to see an insanely handsome man standing behind her. *No such man should happen to a girl when she is emotionally vulnerable,* she thought. The handsome guy was leaning sideways on the bar, looking obliquely at her: dark complexion, clean-shaven, clear jawline, sharp nose, thin lips and deep eyes. Rivanah flashed an abrupt smile which she knew was timed all wrong. A smiling girl emboldens a guy like nothing else. She should have given him a you-talking-to-me glance instead, or better still, no reaction at all.

'Your smile confirms that you indeed are that girl,' the guy said.

'Now you'll say my voice seals it.' The vodka was clearly getting to her head.

'Not if you let me buy you the next drink.' The way his smile redesigned his face took his desirability quotient to temptation level.

'I've already had enough,' she said.

'For tonight, let's presume enough isn't enough.' In the next breath, he called for another drink for her.

In a kinky way, pushy men turned Rivanah on, especially when she was a few vodka shots down. This was one major difference between her former boyfriend Ekansh and Danny: Ekansh would decide for her while the latter would always let her have her way without batting an eyelid. Even now if she stood and flirted with Mr Handsome, she was sure Danny would only smile at her. If it were Ekansh . . . well, she wouldn't have been in the nightclub in the first place.

'Do you always think and speak?' the guy asked.

'Huh?' Before she came across as a dumb person, Rivanah blurted out, 'One more shot and then we hit the floor.'

'Sounds like a plan.'

A minute later the two were grooving to the same number which, minutes back, had irked Rivanah because Nitya and Danny had been dancing to it. She did glance towards them but, as expected, her boyfriend's thumbs-up gesture told her he was happy she too had got someone to dance with. One shouldn't be *this* open-minded, Rivanah told herself, feeling the handsome guy's hands tightening around her waist. With Danny only a few feet away, Rivanah felt uncomfortable with the man's proximity to her, but the disgust triggered in her by Danny's desire to be with Nitya instead of her didn't let the feeling of discomfort last for long. To distract her mind from Danny, she focused on the handsome guy who, she now knew, was looking at her the way a predator looks at a prey. It aroused her.

The handsome guy came close to her and spoke softly into her ears, 'How about we take a stroll outside?' His breath tickled her ears. Rivanah looked at him and nodded. She could do with some fresh air. She didn't care to glance at Danny before stepping out.

The cacophony of the nightclub suddenly vanished the moment they stepped out.

'Do you believe in magic?' the guy asked.

Rivanah thought he was trying to be funny and that she was supposed to laugh. Then she found herself nodding.

'Want to see some now?'

Rivanah nodded again. He smiled at her mischievously and stood facing her. Then slowly he started retreating, one step at a time.

'What are you doing?' she gasped, not knowing what to expect next.

'Wait. And watch.'

Like a teenager, Rivanah waited for some magic trick to unfold itself while watching the handsome guy disappear into the darkness. Then she realized she didn't even know his name. She called out to him only to feel a tap on her back. Rivanah turned in a flash to see the handsome guy standing right behind her, still smiling mischievously.

'What the fuck!' She turned to look at the other end where he had disappeared seconds back and then again at him standing in front of her. She had no clue how he had come behind her so quickly.

'How did you manage to do that?'

'Magic!' the handsome guy said, raising both his hands animatedly in the air.

'Want to see me do it again?'

Rivanah nodded, this time confident she would catch him in the act. The guy yet again started walking backwards from where he stood. Rivanah took a few steps forward, curious to know if there was a shortcut or something but once he disappeared at a distance she knew there was no way he could come up behind her— not this quick. Rivanah kept looking either way eagerly. Half a minute later the handsome guy appeared neither from behind her nor from front, but—to her shock— from inside the nightclub.

'Holy shit!' Rivanah exclaimed.

The guy came up to her and said in a naughty tone, 'I know far more pleasurable magic tricks. Want to give them a try?'

Rivanah knew what he was hinting at: a one-night stand. Something she had never done earlier while involved with Ekansh or Danny. An Audi appeared from nowhere and stopped right in front of her. The front window slowly rolled down. Rivanah bent down to look inside. The same handsome guy who was standing beside her was behind the steering wheel and was also sitting in one of the back seats. *How is that possible?* Before she could decipher if she was hallucinating, Rivanah felt a pair of hands grabbing her from behind. In no time she was bundled into the car by the guy standing beside her. Rivanah found herself sandwiched between the two similar-looking guys while the third drove the Audi.

They were fucking triplets! That seemed like the only plausible explanation.

She tried shouting only to have a hand press her mouth with force. The car was speeding away on the lonely road as she heard the guys tell each other to get her under control. The one who was driving had already switched on some music at top volume to mute her cries. Rivanah was throwing her legs and hands at them in desperation. One of the guys held her hands, while the other held her legs. She tried to move but couldn't. She shouted but it didn't matter. She could now see the two guys looking at her with a sadistic smile. As if her struggle was giving them a kick. Would she able to break free before it was too late? Or was this a nightmare like the ones she had had before? The lusty stares the guys gave her told her otherwise. She felt the will to fight slowly slip away from the grasp of her conscious.

And then the car suddenly came to a halt, throwing everyone in the back seat off balance. The guys beside Rivanah took their hands off her and sat still. Everyone in the car looked out ahead through the windshield. The triplets' faces paled one by one while a bright smile appeared on Rivanah's face. Someone was waiting right in front. Rivanah knew well who this someone could be. He hasn't forgotten me after all, Rivanah thought, feeling relieved. Only *she* knew how much she had missed him all these days . . .

1

Rivanah's parents were pleasantly surprised when she told them she was flying down to Kolkata a fortnight after her call to her mother inquiring about Hiya Chowdhury. This was the first time she was visiting without any apparent reason since she had moved to Mumbai. Rivanah wanted to come down immediately after she spoke to her mother on the phone about Hiya, but she couldn't manage a leave because the client for her project in office was in India. And the first thing she did after her client left was book a flight to Kolkata.

Rivanah hadn't slept properly for over fourteen days. Her mind kept drifting to one single name: *Hiya Chowdhury*. All Rivanah remembered was that Hiya was her batchmate when she was studying engineering. Strangely enough, she remembered the name and even her laughter, but couldn't recall her face. Yet, she was there in her scrapbook. Why was her laughter made to substitute for the normal doorbell in the flat where the stranger supposedly put up? Why were Hiya's interests similar to what the stranger wanted her to do? It was obvious there was a link but what was the link—that was something that stole Rivanah's peace of mind. To add to it, Inspector Kamble, along with the crime branch officer, hadn't been able to trace the stranger after Abhiraj was wrongly nabbed at Starbucks. Most importantly, even the stranger hadn't contacted her in the last fourteen days.

Rivanah's mother was waiting for her on the veranda but, the moment she stepped out of her cab, Rivanah rushed to her room. She didn't even stop to greet her mother.

'*Ki hoyeche ki?*' Before her mother's words could reach her, Rivanah was already in her room upstairs. The first thing she did was go to her study table, kneeling down while pulling the last drawer. What her mother had told her over the phone about Hiya Chowdhury, she had to read for herself. What if her mother had missed something in the scrapbook which was essential in order to track the stranger down or at least activate the link that connected her to Hiya? As Rivanah pulled out almost the entire drawer, a few notebooks fell out of it. She looked thoroughly but there was no scrapbook. She opened the other two drawers above the last but didn't find it there either. She looked on top of her table.

Nothing. She called out to her mother, only to realize she was standing by the door, looking slightly taken aback.

'What are you up to, Mini?' her mother asked.

'Mumma, where's my scrapbook?'

'What book?'

'The one you read to me from, couple of weeks back on the phone? Remember?'

'Oh!' Her mother came inside the room. 'I kept it where it was. Inside the last drawer.'

'But it's not there now!'

Her mother looked as confused as she was.

'But I had kept it here only.'

Rivanah let out a helpless sigh and watched her mother search her table like she had done only seconds back. The result was the same: the scrapbook was not there.

'But why do you need the scrapbook all of a sudden?'

'Nothing.' Rivanah was resigned to her fate. 'Please let me know when you find it,' she said, throwing herself on the bed.

'How long are you staying, Mini?' her mother asked.

'Only this weekend,' Rivanah said, staring at the ceiling. Her mind was elsewhere. It couldn't have been a coincidence that the stranger had saved Hiya's laughter as the doorbell sound in the Mumbai flat. *But why?* Is the stranger related to Hiya? Or is she . . . ? But she only knew

Hiya from college. That's all . . . like she knew so many other students. If she had been close to her she would have at least remembered her face. Perhaps her other friends would have some more information.

'Did you get it, Mumma?' she said, sitting up.

'I'm looking for it.'

For the first time she had had one single lead to who the stranger could be and the scrapbook had gone missing! 'Misplaced', if her mother was to be believed. In the evening, an irritated Rivanah went to the house of her best friend from college, Pooja, in Kalighat. Pooja's marriage was scheduled for the next month but she had come home early to take care of her trousseau and to enjoy her pre-marriage time to the fullest with her parents and siblings. She was delighted to see Rivanah after more than a year.

'You look different, Rivanah!' Pooja exclaimed.

'Really? Like how?'

'I don't know but you do. Come in now.'

The two friends had a lot to catch up on. Pooja had so much to share and so did Rivanah. But all through the conversation, Rivanah kept getting the feeling that she somehow withheld much more than she shared with Pooja. That way she had indeed changed. Over the past year, Rivanah had understood that sharing your emotional woes didn't lead to anything.

'Won't you be working after marriage?' Rivanah asked after she learnt that Pooja had actually resigned from her job.

'I haven't thought about it yet. Right now all I want to do is enjoy this attention that I'm getting from everyone. It is my marriage, after all!'

Rivanah only smiled at her as a reaction.

'Honestly, sometimes I wonder if I even deserve so much happiness. I mean, Rishi and I have been in a relationship from some time now. From the time we first talked to actually marrying him . . . I can't describe it to you, Rivanah. I only want to live this moment as much as I can.'

'It's so important to marry the person you love, isn't it?' Rivanah said.

'Or love the person you marry. I mean, love has to be there.'

'The second option isn't for me and the first I don't know will happen or not,' Rivanah said with a hint of dismay.

'Did you talk to Kaku–Kakima about Danny?'

'I did but talking won't help much I'm afraid. They have a perception and I don't think I'll be able to break it.'

'Think positive,' Pooja said, clasping her friend's hand.

'Remember how Ekansh and I were labelled the fairy-tale couple in college? Everyone thought we were sure to get married. Even we thought so.' A pause later Rivanah added, 'At least *I* thought so.' She broke the clasp and drew her hand back, saying, 'I don't think I'll cry a lot this time. I mean I'll feel bad, maybe I'll be irreversibly damaged too, but still I don't think I will cry if Danny and I don't make the distance, if you know what I mean.'

'No, I don't. What are you saying? Is there any problem between you and . . .'

'Danny is alright. It's just that I haven't been able to move on from Ekansh yet. It's like every day I lie to myself that I have moved on, that I don't love him any more, that it's good that he walked out of our relationship, but whenever I go to bed at night my own lies catch up with me. And mock me in the most painful of ways.'

'Do you really still love Ekansh?' There was a hint of surprise in Pooja's voice which hit Rivanah hard. As if her friend was subtly accusing her: how could you be in love with two people at the same time?

'I have asked myself that question several times but not once have I dared to answer it.'

There was an awkward silence.

'Anyway,' Rivanah said, 'tell me, what do you know about Hiya Chowdhury?'

'Hiya who?'

For a moment Rivanah thought Pooja was kidding. When she had called her right after calling her mother two weeks back, it didn't take her one second to identify Hiya as the girl who had hanged herself.

'Now don't tell me you don't know who Hiya Chowdhury is!'

'Oh, Hiya, yes . . . What about her?' Pooja seemed to remember her, much to Rivanah's relief.

'You tell me anything that I should know about her. I don't remember much really.'

'Anything? What's up with you snooping about Hiya?'

'Why did she die, Pooja?'

The response came a tad later than Rivanah expected.

'How would I know? One day I heard she is no more.'

'She hanged herself from a ceiling fan,' Rivanah said.

'Oh, did she? Poor thing.'

'What poor thing? *You* told me this.'

'I did? Why would I say such a thing when I didn't know it myself?'

'What are you saying?'

Before Pooja could reply, her phone started to ring.

'Rishi is calling. Excuse me, please.'

Pooja went out in the balcony with her phone, leaving Rivanah alone in the room. For the next one hour she didn't come in. Rivanah didn't understand whether she wanted to avoid her or she was actually glued to Rishi's phone call. Rivanah went to the balcony after her patience ran out. Pooja excused herself from Rishi over phone and said, 'I'm so sorry. There's some problem and . . .'

'It's fine. I understand. Let's meet when you are free. I'll be going home now.'

'Okay. Do come for the marriage next month.'

Rivanah nodded and waved her friend goodbye. Seeing Rivanah leave Pooja breathed a sigh of relief. Lying never came naturally to her.

Rivanah went home from Pooja's place and took a nap. At dinner her father surprised her by asking, 'How is Danny?'

Rivanah didn't know if she should be hopeful since her father sounded grumpy rather than concerned.

'He is good, Baba. He was asking about you too.'

'Hmm. Did he bag any film roles?'

'He signed a regional film. Shooting will begin soon.'

'Hmm. And why exactly is Shantu not talking to me?'

This one took Rivanah by surprise. There was a momentary eye-lock with her father and she realized that he knew that Abhiraj was taken into custody.

'Abhiraj was stalking me.'

'You could have told us. Why did you have to go to the police yourself?' Her father's voice rose.

Rivanah was quiet. She knew she couldn't tell him why exactly she had asked the police to butt in.

'Mumma, did you get the scrapbook?' she asked, changing the topic.

'What scrapbook?' Her father was still not done with her.

'I need to know about a friend of mine.'

'Which friend?' her father asked with a frown.

'Hiya Chowdhury.'

Her father's frown went away as he quickly looked away from Rivanah.

'Give me some more rice,' he told his wife and continued, 'You know what happened in office today?'.

2

The next day Rivanah called Pooja inquiring about Hiya's address. Pooja had no idea where Hiya lived or who her close friends were in their batch. Or so she said. Instead of hounding Pooja, Rivanah chose to update her Facebook status: *Guys, remember Hiya Chowdhury? Anyone knows where she lives in Kolkata?*

Three hours later the status had received zero likes, zero comments. Frustrated, Rivanah called up her college. Though it was a Sunday, she knew the college office remained open seven days a week.

'Hello, Techno College? I'm Rivanah Bannerjee; I graduated last year. I'm arranging an alumni meet, so I would like to have the postal addresses of my batchmates to send them invites.'

'That's a lot of names. I can't tell you over the phone. You can come here and collect them for yourself. And please bring your college ID along. Any misuse and you will be responsible.'

'Okay.'

Rivanah reached college within the hour. Though she came with something else in mind, the sight of the college reignited her love story with Ekansh that she had been trying to extinguish for a while now. The good thing was that the emotional embers associated with the memory didn't have any flame, but the bad thing was those embers still had heat left in them. Before those embers could do any further emotional damage, she reached the office. Rivanah was made to wait while her ID was checked. Soon she was given a long printout which had the names and corresponding address of all of her forty-three batchmates. It took little time for her to spot Hiya Chowdhury's name and address. Her house was in Bangur Park in south Kolkata.

Rivanah took a cab from her college in Salt Lake to Bangur Park. She had to ask around a bit to eventually get to Hiya Chowdhury's house. As the cab driver drove away Rivanah turned around to look at the house. She pushed the small iron gate open but couldn't spot anyone or hear any sound coming from inside the house. It was difficult to say if the house was still inhabited. She noticed a white cat atop the terrace looking straight at her and casually moving away as if to inform the owner that someone was here. Rivanah

11

walked to the main door and found that the main door was not locked. She pressed the doorbell. It wasn't the normal ding-dong but had a weird buzz to it. A moment later, the window adjacent to the main door opened.

'Who is it?' asked an elderly man.

'Hello, I'm Rivanah Bannerjee, Hiya's friend.'

'Hiya who?'

'Hiya Chowdhury?'

'You know any Hiya Chowdhury?' The man turned his face away from Rivanah and asked someone inside the house. Rivanah tried to look but couldn't see who it was that the man was talking to.

'Chowdhury? She could be Hiren Chowdhury's daughter,' said a woman who sounded as elderly as the man behind the window.

'They don't live here any more,' the elderly man said, turning towards Rivanah.

'Do you know where—?'

'They were our tenants. These days one doesn't know where one's own children live; how can I tell you about our former tenant's whereabouts?' the elderly man said curtly and shut the window. A moment later she saw the curtains being drawn as well.

So, Hiya Chowdhury and her family lived as tenants here. And if not here then there was no way she could hunt Hiya's family down . . . except if the stranger helped her. It was a dead end as far as Rivanah was concerned. With a heavy heart and a confused mind, she caught a cab once again and went home with two questions clouding her mind. If Hiya was dead and her family was untraceable, why did the stranger lead her to Hiya? And was the scrapbook misplaced by her mother or was it stolen?

Rivanah took a flight back to Mumbai the next morning. While pushing her luggage trolley out of the airport arrival gate, Rivanah's eyes were looking for Danny. He would spring a surprise for her by suddenly appearing with a bunch of roses in his hand and that killer smile of his, she thought, looking around outside the exit gate. There was no sign of Danny.

'Madam, wahan jakar wait kijiye please,' said one of the security personnel by the exit gate, gesturing towards the opposite side. Rivanah didn't even care to look at him as she pushed her trolley. She checked her WhatsApp on the way. She did tell Danny about her flight timings. He should have been there. She called him but there was no answer. The second and third times too the calls were not picked up, though Rivanah held on for the entire ring. With a clogged mind she took a cab straight to Danny's friend's flat in Andheri, Lokhandwala, where she had been living with Danny for about two weeks now. Her parents didn't have a clue about it. Staying all by herself in Mumbai for a little more than a year, Rivanah had learnt that not everyone had to know about everything that happened in one's life. The more you shared your things with people, the more you invite opinion about yourself. She was in love with Danny and was comfortable living with him; that was all that mattered. You are married if you feel you are married. And if you are not, then no ritual can ever make you feel so. Rivanah never tried to explain this to her parents; else they would have taken her to some tantric, accusing her of mental imbalance.

As her cab crossed one traffic signal after another, Rivanah wondered how she had, of late, stopped weighing her relationship with Danny on the weighing scale of marriage. Being with him was more important than any other social licence. The only thing that worried her was that sooner or later her parents would ask her that dreaded question: 'So, what have you decided about marriage?' By then would she be able to muster enough courage to be honest with her parents and tell them that she didn't give a damn about anything except for the fact that she wanted to be with Danny? And he with her.

Once she reached the apartment, she called Danny's phone once again but he still didn't pick up. Going up to the seventh floor in the elevator she checked his last

WhatsApp to her: *Have a safe flight back baby. Love you.* His Last Seen on WhatsApp was when she had boarded the flight.

Rivanah came out of the elevator and dragged her luggage to the main door. In no time she unlocked it with the spare keys. The single lock told her Danny must be at home because he always double-locked the door if outside.

'Hey baby! I'm home,' she yelled.

The response came seconds later. In the voice of a girl.

'Danny is in the shower.'

Rivanah turned around to notice the girl had wet hair, as if she too had been inside the bathroom with . . .

3

'Nitya!' Rivanah said, not sure if she had disguised the fact that she neither expected her in the flat nor did she like it.

'Hi, Rivanah. I'm sorry if I surprised you.'

'I just didn't expect you here,' Rivanah said, putting her luggage down on the floor.

'I know. I also don't want to be here, especially with you and Danny living-in, but you know how Danny is when he gets stubborn. He didn't give me any option,' Nitya said and sat on the plush couch, switching on the television. The indifference with which she sat didn't go well with Rivanah. She knew from before how stubborn Danny could be and it always turned her on emotionally but now she learnt the stubbornness wasn't something exclusive for her. Somewhere within her the realization formed a knot.

'I hope Danny has told you what happened,' Nitya said, her eyes fixed on the television. Rivanah's eyes were fixed on Nitya. What was Danny supposed to tell her about Nitya? Rivanah guessed the worst: Nitya and Danny were a couple now, and she—Rivanah—had been conveniently ousted just as she had been by Ekansh a year back. There was no response for some time. By then Rivanah could feel her guts churning. Danny came out of the bathroom and straight to the drawing room in a vest and knickers, drying his hair with a towel.

'Hey baby! So nice to see you,' said Danny, hugging her and dropped the towel on a beanbag beside her. There's no awkwardness in the hug, Rivanah pondered, something that happens naturally when one emotionally distances oneself from the other. She broke the embrace to look Danny in the eye.

'Were you going to tell me something about Nitya and you?'

Danny shot an incredulous glance at Nitya first and then looking back at Rivanah, said, 'Let's go to the other room.' Danny pulled a bemused Rivanah into the bedroom.

'What is it, Danny? You are scaring me now.'

'Relax. It is not about Nitya and me. It is about Nitya and Nitya only.'

Rivanah gave him a bored look that said 'tell me something new'.

'Nitya had a bad, bad break-up with her boyfriend the day you left for Kolkata. She tried to kill herself. I took her to the hospital and then brought her here. The doctor said she shouldn't be alone right now because she is suicidal.'

Rivanah sighed, trying to ward off all the obnoxious thoughts in her mind and let the fact register in her.

'So, will Nitya stay here with us?' she asked.

Danny nodded.

'For how long?'

'Till she recovers a bit. The doctor said she shouldn't be allowed to stay alone for some time. She is emotionally fragile.'

There was an awkward silence between them. Rivanah didn't want Nitya to stay with them. But she knew if she was honest to Danny it would make her sound rude and he wouldn't appreciate it either. Before she could tell him her decision, Nitya was in the room.

'I'm sorry if I'm disturbing you; if Rivanah has a problem with me staying here, I'm ready to leave. It's really not an issue.'

Danny and Rivanah exchanged a blank look.

'The doctor is mad. I can take care of myself.'

Rivanah went to Nitya and said, 'Why would we have a problem, dear? Please feel free to stay here.'

'Cool,' she said, shooting a look at Rivanah and Danny alternately, and then went away.

'Thank you,' Danny said, wrapping his arms around Rivanah. Only she knew how much pain it caused her to say 'yes' to Nitya. From the day she had first met her a year back, Rivanah never got a vibe from her that said, 'yeah, we can be friends too'.

Hunger pushed Rivanah to quickly change and freshen up. Though she had eaten breakfast on the flight itself, she was famished now since it was past noon by the time she entered her flat. She had already told Danny about how she longed to have a pizza when she reached Mumbai. She joined Danny and Nitya in the drawing room after freshening up and asked which pizza she should order.

'Pizza? But I've already prepared lunch for us,' Nitya exclaimed.

'We can eat that at night,' Rivanah said.

'I was in the kitchen the whole morning preparing salad for us,' Nitya said, which made it seem like she wasn't complaining and yet she was.

'You have the salad, Nitya. Danny and I will surely have it at night.'

'But . . .' Nitya's voice changed gear.

'Can't we have pizza at night?' Danny asked Rivanah. Her jaw would have dropped had she not controlled herself in time.

'Yeah, sure we can,' she said after a moment.

'I'm sure you will like the salad,' Nitya said with a smile and went to the kitchen to fetch it. Rivanah could see a sense of victory in that smile which made her feel uncomfortable. Though Rivanah knew Danny was looking at her, pleading for peace, she chose to look at her phone instead.

For dinner it was pizza indeed but when Rivanah said she wanted to have a Cheese Burst pizza, Nitya said extra cheese gave her a headache. Danny ordered both Cheese Burst as well as a regular one but he ate more from the latter. Rivanah didn't say anything but could feel frustration brewing in her. She ate only one of the six slices and threw the rest in the garbage and she did so exactly when Danny was looking. He didn't probe; she didn't clarify.

Rivanah went to her room, switched off the lights, plugged her ears and listened to a Lana Del Ray song. A few minutes later she felt her earphones being taken off. She didn't have to turn around. She knew it was Danny as his hand rested on her tummy.

'Angry?' he whispered in her ears.

'No,' she said in a stern voice.

'I'm sorry.'

'You don't have to be.'

'Can we go clubbing?'

'Depends on who "we" are.'

'"We" can only mean you and me.'

Rivanah turned to look at him and said, 'Are you sure?'

'Absolutely.'

'Okay.'

'I know you are uncomfortable in Nitya's presence,' Danny said once they were in the car. Somebody had to talk about it. Rivanah was glad it was him.

'I'm not uncomfortable, Danny,' Rivanah said. 'It's just that Nitya and I are two different personalities with different tastes. And you know that. Personally I don't have a problem with Nitya but . . .'

'But . . . ?'

But . . . your closeness to her burns me. Rivanah wondered how she could dress this naked truth in a way that it didn't make her sound insecure.

Danny shrugged at her, still seeking closure.

'But . . . nothing,' Rivanah said.

'It's just a matter of a few days.'

'Hmm.' Rivanah turned the stereo on and rolled down the window to get some fresh air. Danny switched off the AC and asked, 'Anything about Hiya Chowdhury?'

Rivanah gave him a sharp glance and then, leaning back on the seat while looking outside, said, 'Nothing. I tracked down where she used to live but nobody from

21

her family lives there any more. It was a rented place. The owners too don't know where the Chowdhury family has moved to after Hiya's death.'

'And did she really die just the way you envisioned in your nightmares?'

'Yes. Pooja said Hiya died after hanging herself from the ceiling fan.' *But Pooja also acted funny, saying she didn't remember saying so.* Rivanah didn't share this with Danny.

Danny put his hand on hers. He tightened his grasp as she gave him a relaxed smile. It was a cool night with low traffic. She leaned sideways and kissed him on his cheeks and then licked her way to his ears. The car wobbled on the road.

'Control, baby,' Danny said. Both had a naughty smile on their faces. Before they could take things one step further, his phone rang. Since the phone was lying on the deck, Rivanah could easily read the name of the caller: Nitya. She pushed the phone towards Danny and rested on her seat again. Danny slowed down as he took the call. The next second he took a U-turn.

'What happened?' Rivanah asked.

'Nitya has high fever. We have to go back.'

The concern in his voice saddened her. She knew as a friend he ought to be concerned but what was she to feel, as a girlfriend, about this? No, as an *insecure* girlfriend. Danny didn't say a single word as he drove fast to their apartment. Once there Rivanah stayed back in the car as he rushed to the flat. Sitting in the car she wanted to tell someone her point of view. That she wasn't a bitch who didn't care if a person had high fever but . . . she unlocked her phone, tapped on Contacts and went to a name that read Stranger.

She typed a message: *Please tell me you are there*. She sent it but she didn't get a delivery report. She chose to wait.

4

Rivanah woke up to the sound of the doorbell. She looked around and found herself in her room. At first, all she remembered was sitting inside the car. Then she remembered how even after half an hour the message to the stranger had not been delivered. She had come back to the flat last night to see Danny checking the thermometer while Nitya lay on the couch. Rivanah hadn't bothered to ask anything.

Rivanah got up, tied her hair into a loose bun and went to open the door. There were two pouches of milk on the ground. She picked it up and locked the main door. It was then that her eyes fell on Danny who was asleep on the couch while Nitya's head rested on his lap; she too was asleep. There was nothing objectionable in it and yet there was something deeply disturbing. She wanted to wake them up immediately but, she wondered, why did Danny have to make Nitya sleep on his lap? Rivanah understood she was his best friend but she wasn't his girlfriend. There's a difference. *Is there?* Rivanah thought and stopped herself from waking them up. *Can a guy's girl best friend and girlfriend live together with him?* With this question probing her calmness, Rivanah went to take a shower instead of sleeping for a few minutes more.

When she stepped out of the shower, she noticed Nitya was preparing tea for herself in the kitchen while Danny was on the phone. When the call ended, he joined her in the bedroom.

'I have an important audition today for a movie,' he said, putting his arms around her from behind, trying to be cosy with her. She could still feel the coldness with which he had left her in the car last night. From that coldness to this cosiness—how was she supposed to adjust so quickly and that too with no explanation or even a whisper of an apology?

'I thought you would come to the room after Nitya slept,' she said, shrugging her shoulders a bit as if she didn't appreciate his arms around her at the moment.

Danny looked as if he was expecting something else from Rivanah.

'I dozed off. Why do you ask?'

Was she wrong in expecting an apology from him because he didn't come to his girlfriend's room at night?

'Nothing,' Rivanah said. 'When is your audition?'

'They wanted me to be there in the morning itself but I have rescheduled it for the evening.'

'Why? You have another one in morning?'

'No. I need to take Nitya to the doctor. She still has fever.'

Rivanah gave him a momentary glance and, turning her back to him said, 'I'll take her to the doctor. You go to the audition.'

Danny wrapped his arms around her once again from behind, this time tighter, and said, 'I love you.'

'Me too,' she said, removing his arms immediately. Only she knew that she had proposed to take Nitya to the doctor out of her own sense of insecurity. Pistanthrophobia was the word—the fear of trusting someone because of a previous bad experience. Thanks to Ekansh, Rivanah could think of nothing else but the fact that every girl in her man's life was a potential threat to her relationship. The closer the girl to your partner, the more active the threat was. Whether Danny was lured by Nitya or he fell for her, the result would be same: Rivanah would be single. She had suffered such a thing before. And somewhat recovered, if not fully. But if it happened again—just one more time—then nothing in this world would be able to cure her. People don't understand but heartbreak, with time, becomes a disease, a well-kept secret disease whose symptom is a deep mistrust, and that is incurable. She promised herself that she would do her part at least so that what happened between Ekansh and her didn't happen again. And thus she decided to take Nitya to the doctor.

Danny dropped both Rivanah and Nitya at the doctor's and drove off to his audition. It took close to an hour before they were done with the check-up. As they came out Rivanah called for a Tab cab. When it arrived, Nitya persuaded Rivanah to head to her office while she went home alone.

Once in office Rivanah's team lead, Sridhar, told her something which instantly filled her with excitement.

'There's an on-site opportunity coming up for two of our team members and I will be forwarding your name.'

'You mean I will go to London?'

'Yes, if selected, you'll have to work from there for two years.'

'Wow! Thank you so much.' Rivanah was genuinely thrilled. She had worked hard on the project and finally it was time for her reward. She immediately called Danny but he didn't pick up. Then she called her mother who was equally jubilant hearing this. Rivanah knew her mother would inform every close and distant relative of theirs about this in no time. After all Rivanah would be the first woman in her family to work abroad. The rest had only tagged along with their husbands on a dependant visa.

A few minutes after her mother had put the phone down, Rivanah got a call from Danny.

'Sorry, baby. I was driving.'

'It's okay. I guessed so.' Rivanah was about to share the good news when she heard Danny say, 'I'm back home.'

'Huh? Why?' The smile disappeared from Rivanah's face. A frown appeared instead.

'Some crisis came up at the production office. The audition will possibly happen tomorrow.'

'So?'

'So, I'll be at home only.'

'Oh. Okay.' Rivanah was lost. *He was at home. So was Nitya.*

'You called me, right?' Danny said.

'Yeah. Just like that.'

'Okay. Let's talk later then. I need to give Nitya some medicine.'

'Yeah, sure. Bye,' Rivanah said and cut the call. She had a constant frown from then on. Physically she was in the office with her team but mentally she was at her flat wondering what Danny and Nitya were up to. She called Danny half an hour later.

'Hey, what's up?' he said.

'Nothing. Was missing you. What are you doing?'

'I was shaving.'

'And Nitya?'

'She is sleeping. It's the side effect of the medicines.'

'Okay.'

Was Nitya really sleeping? Rivanah cut the call, feeling ashamed for doubting Danny's words. She went back to work but still couldn't focus. A restlessness caught up with her; she drank water from time to time, took deep breaths and tried to distract herself, but failed miserably. She called Danny again after twenty minutes. And again. And again.

'What's up with you today? Don't you have any work in the office?' Danny said when he picked up her call for the fifth time in an hour and a half.

'Why, aren't you happy I'm calling you?'

'I'm not.'

'Huh?'

'I would rather have you home if you are out of work,' Danny giggled.

'What's Nitya doing?'

'She is taking a shower.'

'Okay.'

'Listen, thanks,' Danny said.

'For?'

'For being so concerned about Nitya. I know I didn't discuss it with you before I brought her here but I'm so happy with the way you embraced the whole situation.'

Rivanah could have choked to death hearing this. She only swallowed a lump, sitting on her chair in her cubicle, trying hard to pretend she didn't hear what Danny said.

'There?' Danny said.

'Yes. Let me call you later. Team lead's calling. Bye.' Rivanah cut the phone and kept it in her bag, promising herself she wouldn't call Danny again that day.

Just before she was about to leave for the day, Sridhar told her to keep her passport ready.

'Sure. I'll let you know when done.'

She couldn't wait to share the news with Danny. And when she did tell him after she reached home, Danny was equally excited.

'I'm really happy for you. But I'll miss you as well,' Danny said, hugging her tight. It was then that Rivanah realized what she had forgotten the whole time. It made her jittery. And somewhat neurotic too. What if Danny and Nitya continued to live together after she shifted to London?

'You'll come with me,' she said and immediately knew it was stupid of her to say that. Danny half broke the embrace to look at her and said, 'How I wish!'

Rivanah managed a tight smile.

'May I say something?' Nitya barged in. Danny and Rivanah together turned around to see Nitya leaning by the room's door. They awkwardly broke their embrace completely. Nitya looked at Rivanah and said, 'Don't worry. In your absence, I shall take proper care of him.' She gave Rivanah a warm smile. It hit her like a poisoned arrow.

Rivanah couldn't sleep that night even though, unlike the previous night, Danny was right next to her, sound asleep. The same relationship, Rivanah pondered, which had made her sniff freedom months back was pushing her to limit her career choice. With her in London and Nitya taking care of Danny, she wouldn't be surprised if their relationship ballooned into love. And if that balloon started flying high she would never be able to catch it and burst it. Who would she blame then: Danny or herself? Rivanah longed to talk to someone about this. She checked the messages on her phone once. Her message to the stranger still hadn't been delivered. Was he gone forever? Why did he come in the first place? Why was Hiya Chowdhury's laughter so important that he used it as a doorbell sound? Would she never know about it at all? Thoughts about Danny and Nitya, the stranger and Hiya started intermingling in her mind, creating a jumble. Out of sheer frustration she sent the same message she did a day back to all the numbers she had saved of the stranger, and closed her eyes to think: she had never been a career-oriented girl. All she needed was someone who loved her truly. And now when she had one, was it worth risking it all to go to London to work?

At four in the morning she sat up on her bed, took her phone and typed a message for her team lead: *Hi Sridhar, sorry to message you this late. I had a talk with my parents. I won't be able to get my passport in the next three months. I think I'll let this opportunity go by. Sorry.*

After sending it she checked her messages to the stranger once again. None were delivered. She called those numbers. None of them were switched on . . . yet.

5

Returning from her office, Rivanah got down from the autorickshaw at the start of the lane which led to her building. As she walked down the lane she realized it was unusually quiet. The adjoining shops were shut; some of the street lights were also not working while the street dogs which usually hovered around were missing. She checked her watch: 7.30 p.m. She wondered what was wrong and walked on. The moment she reached the end of the lane, she realized what was wrong. She had reached the same spot she had got out at. *How is it possible?* She turned with a fear slowly rising in her, which made her run towards the other end. She reached the spot only to realize it was the same place where she started from. She kept running from one end of the lane to the other in a loop, unable to find her building. Rivanah was sweating by now, perplexed at what was happening. She screamed for help but there was nobody around. As she for the umpteenth time tried to run to the other end, hoping to find her building this time, she noticed one of the street lights was on. Its light fell directly on a grilled manhole. And from inside it a hand came up. Accompanying the hand was a voice.

'Help me, Rivanah. Help me. I'm trapped.'

She didn't recognize the voice. With unsteady steps Rivanah reached the manhole. And through the grill saw her own self trapped inside. But as her own self saw her peeping, her visage changed into a demonic one that cried out, 'I'll get you, Rivanah. Soon, I'll get you.'

Rivanah's eyes snapped open. After a long time the nightmare had returned. Sleep had been a far cry for Rivanah ever since coming back to Mumbai the previous weekend; she didn't know when she had dozed off that night. She quickly gulped some water from the bottle by her side and, lowering the AC temperature by three degrees with the remote, she tried to close her eyes and relax. She found her mind working even more maliciously, all the while knitting imaginary tales involving Danny and Nitya. As if her mind had nothing else to think about. When did she become so insecure? She knew that the chances of Danny leaving her for Nitya were negligible but the thought still bothered her a great deal.

Rivanah sat up. Danny was sound asleep beside her. She caressed his hair. He didn't budge. Their love story wasn't a smooth one. She knew she had to still convince

34

her parents about him but she was ready to fight it out. But this new problem, the root of which lay deep within her—she didn't know how to uproot it. Rivanah felt choked looking at the calm edpression on Danny's face. She would have burst into tears if she had not withdrawn herself away from him right at that moment.

She went and drew the curtain of the window to inhale the fresh morning air. Dawn had just broken. She looked down and noticed a jogger on the footpath. On an impulse she put on her tracksuit, got into her Converse shoes, tied her hair in a bun and looked at herself in the mirror. It was the same tracksuit she had worn to the gym when she was trying to woo Danny last year. A tiny smile touched her face. Things had moved so fast. Her thoughts shifted to how Ishita and she had tried to woo Danny together and how miserably the former had failed. Ishita was the only one whom she could call a friend in Mumbai other than Danny, but she had shifted to Gurgaon following a new job. And all that remained of that friendship was a Like and a Comment on each other's Facebook update.

Rivanah felt the morning air work as an elixir as she started jogging on the lonely road right in front of her apartment. At least the motion of jogging took her mind off the garbage she had been pondering over almost all day and night. Rivanah slowed down on seeing a young girl running towards her. She wasn't wearing a tracksuit and the way she was running told Rivanah she was in some kind of trouble. She waited for the girl to come close to her. The girl stopped right beside Rivanah.

'Didi, please help me!' the girl said, gasping for air.

'Relax! What happened?'

'I have a job interview and I live far from this place. Hence I left home early. But these two boys have been following me and . . .' The girl looked towards the end of the street where Rivanah, following her eyes, realized two guys in a bike had taken a turn. Rivanah looked around. She spotted an autorickshaw approaching.

'Quick!' Rivanah pulled the girl by her arm and in a flash stopped the autorickshaw and climbed in. The driver looked at her expectantly.

'Police station!' she said. The autowallah took a U-turn and accelerated. Rivanah peeped out and realized the guys would catch up with them before they reach the police station.

'What do you have in that bag?' Rivanah asked the girl who immediately opened the bag and showed it to her. There was a tiffin box, a file, a deodorant, a few cosmetics, a hairbrush and an umbrella. Rivanah took out the umbrella and pulled its stem out without opening it. This time she didn't have to peep out. The guys on the bike had closed in on the autorickshaw. The autowallah asked them to behave only to be rebuked in the dirtiest of cuss words. The guy riding pillion shouted to the one driving the bike that now they had two girls—one for his friend and one for him. They laughed in a lurid manner. The autowallah drove away from the bike but Rivanah asked the driver to take the auto close to the bike once more. Once that was done, she smiled at the guys, taking them by surprise, and then shoved the umbrella between the spikes of the bike's back wheel. The umbrella immediately broke but by then the bike and the guys on it were all over the road. They hurled abuses at Rivanah as the autowallah sped past them.

'Thank you so much. I hope you are not hurt,' the girl said, sounding extremely relieved.

Rivanah had felt a strong jerk in her hand but it was nothing serious.

'Fear is the most prized illusion we create for ourselves, dear. Never be afraid of such louts. They feed on our fear,' Rivanah said. A smile of realization touched her face. These were the same words the stranger had once written on one of the embroidered white cloths he had sent her.

'I'll always remember that,' the girl said. Rivanah got off the auto at the closest traffic signal, asked the driver to drop the girl at her destination, and jogged back to her apartment. She did notice a few men trying to get the two bikers to hospital but she didn't care to stop. *Next time they would remember not to harass a girl on the road,* she thought, and jogged on. While moving into her apartment building she realized that if this incident had happened two years back she would have never been able to help the girl the way she did this morning. The guts, the attitude, the confidence to tackle the situation had developed in her since the last year . . . since the stranger had come into her life. In a way, the stranger had become a part of her system. She might fear him but she wouldn't be able to sever herself from him. He was the one who had unlocked a secret Rivanah hidden within herself: a Rivanah who knew how to stand up and pack a punch.

She went to her flat, showered and was ready for office. By then even Danny and Nitya were ready. The latter had of late started working as an assistant to a famous stylist who had ample links in the film industry. There was a rehearsal for a show which was supposed to be attended by a top-notch film director and thus Danny had the right reason to tag along with Nitya. The fact that Nitya worked at a place where Danny could seek his professional break made Rivanah feel like an outcast. She was in IT and there was no reason why

Danny would ever tag along with her to her office. She didn't say much and stepped out before they did, wishing Danny luck.

In the office Rivanah didn't call Danny even once. Nor did a call or message come from him. Though it was usual for Danny to not call her when he was out for work, it made Rivanah feel uneasy. Five times that day she picked up her phone, almost tapping the Call button against his name, but she somehow didn't. She could feel a restlessness building up inside her but it couldn't locate a vent in the form of a person. In the evening she called her mother.

'Hello, Mumma.'

'Mini? What happened? Why are you calling at this time? Everything's fine?'

'Why, can't I call you just like that?'

'Of course you can. But you generally call around eight in the evening.'

Rivanah talked with her mother for the next fifteen minutes. Many a time she thought of sharing her fear about Danny with her mother, but realized there came a time when you couldn't share everything with your mother, no matter how close she was to you. *Being a grown up, you have to drink your poison yourself,* she thought. Was it time for her to accept the fact that, at twenty-three, she was a lonely soul? Something she had never thought was possible in her wildest dreams. In the evening Rivanah went to a lonely flat, had a lonely supper because Danny was still out and she didn't care where Nitya was. At around eleven at night she got a call from Danny asking her to come to Hype, a nightclub in Bandra. Just when she thought she would have to resign to her inner loneliness, there was a spark of hope. Rivanah dressed up quickly and took a cab to Hype. And there she saw Danny and Nitya waiting for her.

'Tomorrow is Nitya's birthday. So I thought we'll celebrate it here itself,' Danny said and realized the surprise wasn't well received by Rivanah. Nitya excused herself to go to the washroom and he tried to explain, 'Baby, I know I didn't tell you about this before. And trust me, if Nitya wasn't single and hadn't done the shit she tried to do, I wouldn't have done this . . .' Rivanah didn't bother to hear the rest.

'It's okay, Danny,' she said.

They cut the cake at midnight. Rivanah not only had to force herself to smile constantly but also had to click a lot of pictures of Danny and Nitya where both were either hugging or the latter kissing the former's cheek or, worse, had to pose between Danny and Nitya with the latter clicking their selfies. Once they were done with the photos, Nitya asked her, 'May I ask your boyfriend for a dance?'

Rivanah was pissed off but nodded with a tight smile. As they danced, she went to the bar with a mild headache. She ordered her drink and considered going back home when she heard a man's voice.

'You remind me of someone.'

She was emotionally vulnerable and his timing was right. To add to it he was drop-dead handsome. She couldn't resist the urge to accompany him on the dance floor. She hoped Danny would leave Nitya and come to her, at least out of jealousy. He didn't. In fact he flashed a smile at her which infuriated her and made her desperate to get out of the place.

'Do you mind taking a stroll with me outside?' the handsome guy spoke in her ears. It was like he read her mind. Rivanah instantly agreed.

Outside, she felt better till the handsome guy showed her a magic trick she wasn't prepared for. Excusing himself, he went away and then appeared right behind her. Then he went backwards, disappearing at the bend of the road and reappearing in front of her. Rivanah stood awed at what was happening. Next a car came and stopped right in front of her. The handsome guy was beside her, inside the car by the steering and sitting in the back seat as well—all at the same time. By the time she understood they were triplets she was pushed into the car. The loud music from the car's stereo muted her cries. She fought hard but before her fear paralysed her to surrender herself to the look-alike beasts, the car came to a screeching halt. The three looked in front of the car. The triplets' faces paled one by one while a bright smile appeared on Rivanah's face. There was a jeep in front of them. A siren was flashing above it. Two policemen were standing by the jeep. One of the triplets started backing their car but was soon sandwiched by a police vehicle from behind. Four policemen—two from each vehicle—came towards the car and knocked on the darkened windshield. By then the two guys had let go of Rivanah inside the car. She unlocked the door and got out, almost kicking out one of the guys who looked as if he had peed in his pants. The policemen took the three guys inside one of their jeeps. Rivanah meanwhile kept looking all around as if she knew *he* had to be around.

'Are you all right, madam?' asked one of the policemen.

'Yes. Who informed you?' Rivanah asked, still looking around.

'Someone named Hiya Chowdhury,' said the policeman.

6

Fate is a smell, Mini. Follow it hard and you shall reach me.

Rivanah had kept all the white cloths she had received embroidered with the messages from the stranger in her cupboard, with the last one on top. The message . . . Hiya's laughter on the doorbell . . . her nightmares . . . these were the dots which she had not been able to connect at all. And before she could ask the stranger about it he had vanished from her life.

Last night when the policeman had mentioned the name Hiya Chowdhury, her jaw had dropped. But the answer to her next question revealed the reality.

'Did she say anything else?'

'She? It was a man.'

And Rivanah realized who it could be.

'What did he look like?' she asked.

'We only received a call at our control room. The details say it was Hiya Chowdhury, a fifty-year-old man living in Byculla. The address is . . .'

Rivanah didn't bother to listen. It had to be a wrong address. But the phone call also meant the stranger had been keeping an eye on her like always, though without making his presence felt. On the one hand she didn't know why he had become so dormant suddenly—was it due to the police threat?—while on the other hand she was happy too, because she suddenly knew she wasn't as lonely as she thought. The stranger was around . . . somewhere near her. Rivanah didn't tell Danny about the incident right then. One of the police jeeps had dropped her back at the nightclub. It was the next night, when Danny and she retired to bed, that she said, 'What will make you jealous, Danny?'

'What do you mean?' Danny was lying sideways, looking at her, resting his head on his hand.

'How did you feel when you saw me dancing with a guy the other night?' Rivanah was lying on her back, looking at nothing specific on the ceiling.

'How am I supposed to feel when you were having a good time?'

'But I wasn't having that good time with you.'

'But you were having a good time, right?'

The fact that Danny still didn't get what she was trying to imply irked her. *Don't you get it, Danny?! I was jealous seeing Nitya and you dance,* Rivanah framed in her mind how she would say it, *and I don't want to see the two of you together again, no matter how much of an emotional catastrophe she is in.*

'Yes, I was having a good time,' Rivanah said aloud. She didn't know why she suddenly couldn't be honest about her feelings with him. Was it because, if she said it, there was a possibility that Danny would judge her? Or was it because she judged her own self?

'What happened? You sound disconnected.' Danny placed his hand across her bosom.

'How long will Nitya stay here?'

Danny understood the subtext of the query. He came closer and said, 'A few more days. Once her medication is over and the doctor tells me it is okay for her to stay alone, everything will be the way it was before.'

'Promise?'

Danny planted a soft kiss on her forehead and said, 'Promise. But I'm sure you will agree she isn't much of a trouble.'

Rivanah took her time before she said, 'Yeah.' She turned towards him and both of them closed their eyes together. After some time Rivanah opened hers and kept staring at Danny as if she was trying to understand herself by looking at him. She had no idea when she fell asleep.

The next day Nitya had to shop for some outfits for the stylist she was working for. She was heading from her stylist's office in Andheri to Phoenix Mall in Lower Parel. She called Danny to ask if he could drop her. He agreed to. Just prior to that Rivanah had called him for lunch at Indigo Deli in Andheri. Danny called her and asked if she could come down to Phoenix instead.

'Phoenix? That's so far from my office. Indigo is fine, Danny.'

'Actually Nitya needs to buy some stuff and she doesn't know the place well and I'm free so . . .'

Rivanah suddenly found she had no option. She could have asked Danny to skip meeting Nitya and meet her in Indigo instead, but she knew there would be numerous calls from Nitya which would make Danny rush through the lunch and leave even before she was halfway through hers.

'Let's meet at Phoenix,' Rivanah said resignedly. She immediately excused herself from her team leader saying she wasn't feeling well and had to go to a doctor. Sridhar let her leave for the day. Of late, he had found her focus at work wavering. He wanted to tell her that he found her sudden unwillingness to go on-site rather weird, and would have actually tried to convince her against her decision, if he didn't have other equally qualified contenders ready to pounce on the opportunity.

Rivanah joined Danny in Andheri after which they picked up Nitya from her office. Then together they headed towards Phoenix Mall. Though Rivanah tried to help Nitya choose the dresses she needed, Nitya's queries were all directed towards Danny. Soon she got tired of butting in with her opinion. The way Danny's suggestions were appreciated by Nitya hurt Rivanah even though she knew it was possible they weren't intended to hurt her. It was the language of insecurity that made her read their behaviour in one particular dimension only. While Danny was involved in suggesting something to Nitya, Rivanah took a couple of steps back. She saw that Danny didn't even notice it; he was so engaged with Nitya. Then Rivanah went outside the store and looked at them through the glass from a distance. The indifference in Danny triggered a sudden and strong urge in her to get his attention. As if that was the only relief she knew of to the itch that her insecurity had become. She looked around casually trying to think of a plan of action to make Danny run to her. Soon she knew what exactly she had to do.

Rivanah headed towards the lingerie section in an adjacent multipurpose store and picked up three bras and three matching G-strings. She went into one of the trial rooms and quickly stripped off her kurti and leggings and her bra. She put on the purple-coloured bra which she had brought with her and clicked a selfie with a pout. She WhatsApped the picture to Danny immediately and waited desperately for him to come online on the app. Half a minute later, he was online. He messaged back: *Where are you?* Rivanah had a mischievous smile on her face. Next she sent a picture of herself in the purple G-string. Danny immediately called up on seeing the picture. She cut the line without answering, smiling all the while. She then sent him yet another picture wearing another set of lingerie. This time when he called her, she picked up and in one breath said, 'The adjacent store, first trial room. I'm waiting.' Within seconds she could hear footsteps coming towards her. Then she looked down. From below the door she could see a shadow moving close to the trial room. On an impulse she unlocked the trial room's door and pulled Danny in by his tee. Before he could speak her lips were on his. His hands were on her butt over her G-string while hers were cupping his face. She smooched him with a deep passion that emboldened Danny to get into the act as well.

'I didn't tell Nitya that—' Danny tried to break off from the smooch for a moment to speak but Rivanah kissed him again. As their tongues slurped each other's his squeeze on her buttocks tightened. In a flash her hand was at his groin and he felt her hand massaging his semi-erect penis over his jeans. Danny had never seen such aggressive sexual behaviour in Rivanah before. On the one hand it aroused him and on the other he was worried about Nitya since he had rushed off without telling her. Danny wanted to break free but he heard Rivanah say, 'Suck me, baby.' And all he could do was rip off her bra and take her right breast in his mouth, sucking hard at the light-brown areola. Rivanah's eyes were shut tight. It had been some time since they had made love. The urgency of it only excited the sexual flame within. Their kiss broke for a moment and there was a sudden eye-lock.

'Fuck me, Danny,' Rivanah rasped.

Danny quickly unzipped, took out his fully erect penis and pulled the string of her G-string. It dropped to the ground. He turned her. Rivanah could now see both of them in the mirror in front. Her own self never aroused her more than it did at that moment. Danny slowly inserted his penis in her wet vagina. A moan escaped her. He was about to start his thrusts when they heard something: Nitya was calling out to Danny in a helpless, forlorn tone.

'Damn! I knew it,' Danny mumbled under his breath, sounding worried and crossed. He pulled out of her instantly.

'Danny! Finish what you started,' Rivanah said. But he paid no attention. In no time Danny was outside the trial room. A highly frustrated Rivanah didn't move for some time. She looked at herself in the mirror. A loser was staring back at her. She took a deep breath and then put on her dress. She went out only to see Nitya crying profusely, holding on to Danny in a tight embrace, resting her head on his chest and telling him that she thought he too had left her like her boyfriend. Rivanah didn't know what to make of it. The salesgirl who had taken Rivanah to the trial room came to her with an annoyed expression. Rivanah gave her a hundred-rupee note for allowing Danny inside the trial room. The moment she did so Rivanah heard Danny shout out Nitya's name. The latter had fainted.

In the hours that followed, Danny rushed Nitya to the doctor with Rivanah quietly accompanying him. She had never seen Danny as worried and tense as he was in those few hours. It scared her because she wasn't the subject of his worry. Rivanah knew she was being acutely selfish but she didn't know what to do if not be herself. The doctor found that Nitya's blood pressure had fallen. She was admitted to a nursing home for some time. By evening she seemed fine. It was the same doctor who had treated Nitya after her failed suicide attempt. He was angry with Danny for being negligent and strictly asked him to keep her out of any kind of emotional turmoil. While taking Nitya back home, Rivanah asked Danny if they should inform Nitya's parents about her condition. Danny gave her a stern look. It was only when they reached home and Nitya was asleep that Danny spoke to Rivanah.

'Nitya doesn't have a father. And she isn't in touch with her mother because her mother married her husband's business partner, which Nitya didn't like. So all she has right now is me.'

They were in the drawing room while Nitya had been put to bed in their room.

'Oh! I never knew that.'

'But you knew that she is emotionally unstable right now, didn't you?' he said, glaring at her.

Rivanah was taken aback by his accusatory tone.

'I did. So?'

'So what was the need for that stupidity?'

'What stupidity?' Only her mouth was moving. The rest of Rivanah was pretty tense.

'Calling me into the trial room?'

'When did I call you?'

'Yeah? Why else did you send me your hot pics?'

'I just wanted to share them with you, Danny. Am I not allowed to do that?'

'Of course you are allowed to. But why did you have to do it when I was with Nitya? You didn't even tell me before you went to the other store.'

'Since when do I have to take your permission before doing something?'

'It's not that. All I mean is just don't make it tough for me.'

'Tough for *you*? Do you know how tough it has been for me since I came back from Kolkata and saw Nitya putting up here?'

'Why would it be tough for you?'

'If my best friend was a guy and I brought him here to stay with us for whatever reason, then wouldn't it be tough for you?' Rivanah felt she could cry any moment. Their spat was fast taking a dangerous turn.

'Nitya isn't here for whatever reason. I think I told you already but it seems you didn't listen properly or try to understand. But now I'm saying it again. Nitya tried to kill herself!' Danny raised his pitch to an extent that jolted her. He had never spoken to her in such a high-pitched tone before. It reminded Rivanah of her cousin Meghna and Aadil. That, she knew, was bad news.

'Why are you shouting at me, Danny?'

'Because I have tried to be gentle and you still haven't got the point.'

'What's the point?'

'The point is Nitya is not well and we shouldn't be selfish.'

'Even if it eats into our relationship?'

Danny gave her a searching look and said, 'Till now it hasn't. But only till now. If you continue to behave like an imbecile then it very well may,' Danny said and walked out of the flat, leaving Rivanah in tears. She felt weak from within, just like she did when she had seen Ekansh with another girl a year back. Only this time she feared this weakness could be irreversible. She somehow managed to stumble towards the couch and collapsed on it, sobbing hard. This dreaded moment where she was made to feel like a loser wasn't alien to her. With Ekansh she didn't see it coming while with Danny she tried her best to prevent it, and yet here she was in the middle of it, all alone. Why was she alone? Wasn't there anyone who could understand why she did what she did? Someone who would say she did the right thing and that Danny was the one being insensitive? Someone who would not judge her but appreciate the fact that anyone in her place would have done and felt the same and whatever she was going through was absolutely normal? Absolutely human? She knew who that someone was . . .

But the question was, where was that someone?

7

Danny came back around two at night. He had his own set of keys so Rivanah didn't have to open the door. With Nitya sleeping in their room, Rivanah was lying down on the sofa-cum-bed. The moment she heard the door unlock, she turned around and feigned sleep. She had left ample amount of space for Danny to sleep beside her but he chose to sit on the beanbag instead. She didn't sleep a wink the entire night. By morning she had had enough. Rivanah called all the phone numbers she had stored of the stranger but found all of them still out of service. Earlier maybe it was a luxury for her to connect to the stranger but overnight it had become a need. And a burning need at that.

That day Rivanah went to office with an idea of how to connect with the stranger. Perhaps the only one she knew with whom she could talk, exposing her naked emotional self. She designed a fake document about some fictitious astrological guru with some fake numbers, took a printout and then made exactly fifty-four photocopies of it. There were fifty-five flats in Krishna Towers where she lived in Lokhandwala. When she returned from office in the evening she went to each and every flat with the photocopied pamphlet to hand it over to the residents herself. The real intention was to know if there was any flat which was locked for the world outside but inhabited secretly, just like it was when she lived in Sai Dham Apartments in Goregaon East. To her dismay there was not a single flat that was locked up. Every flat either had families or couples living in it. The probability of the stranger living with a family seemed farfetched to Rivanah. She confidently concluded that the stranger wasn't living in Krishna Towers. And yet the nightclub incident with the triplets was proof enough that he was keeping an eye on her. What was stopping him from contacting her? Could it be . . . ? She finally thought she had got the answer.

Rivanah went to the Goregaon police station. Inspector Kamble who had been helping her with the case seemed more than happy to see her.

'Miss Bannerjee. How are you?'

She found it sweet that he still remembered her.

'I'm fine, sir. How are you?'

'I'm good too. My daughter finally got a placement here in Mumbai. Such a relief it is.'

'That's wonderful!' Rivanah was genuinely happy for him.

'What brings you here? Though I'm sorry nothing has come up about that person who was stalking you.'

'It's okay. I want to take back my complaint.'

'As in, you want me to close the case?' Kamble was taken aback.

'Yes.'

'Why?'

'I don't think the person will disturb me again,' Rivanah said. Her main purpose was something else. And she hoped Kamble wouldn't outsmart her by deciphering it.

'Hmm. As you say. But do let me know if anything comes up.'

'I surely will, sir. Thank you so much.'

Rivanah was made to sign a couple of documents after which she was getting up to leave when Kamble spoke up, 'I want you to suggest something to me on a personal level.'

'Sure.'

Kamble too stood up and said, 'Come.' He led her outside the police station where he stood with her and said, 'Suppose you have chosen someone as your life partner and your parents aren't sure about it, then what should your parents do so you don't get angry with them?'

For a moment Rivanah thought Kamble was asking about her own self.

'I'm asking this because my daughter has a boyfriend whom I don't like, but she says she wants to marry him. I thought, since you are of her age, perhaps you could help me understand how youngsters think.'

'I think you should accept her choice. After all, your daughter has to live with her choice, you don't. So let her have her way. Good or bad, she will have to live with her decision,' Rivanah said, wishing someone would suggest the same thing to her father as well.

'Hmm. Thank you.'

Rivanah exited the police station and looked around for an autorickshaw. She was sure the stranger was watching her. If he could know so much about her then he would also know she had taken her case back. If the police was the reason he was hiding, he better show up now. She climbed into an autorickshaw, burning with curiosity.

Her cold war with Danny continued. She was yet to forgive him for leaving her sexually frustrated the other day. Though she didn't bring it up with him, she hadn't forgotten it. Rivanah didn't say anything when she saw him leave with Nitya. Instead of going to work in the morning, Rivanah went to Dahisar where she used to teach the ten kids: *Mini's Magic 10*. She did visit the place a day after Abhiraj was wrongly caught as the stranger. But she didn't find any kids there then. She asked around but she couldn't get a lead. Her only consolation was that she had done her part by then. She had shared her good luck . . . the kids had learnt to write basic English. Standing near the space where her classes used to take place, she couldn't locate any of the kids. In its place stood a tiny grocery store now. Perhaps the stranger had put those ten kids in some school somewhere as he had once told her he would. Rivanah stayed there for some time, keeping an eye out for any kid entering the place. A few did turn up but none were from the ten she had taught. Though she was crestfallen, standing under the sun and looking around, she somehow felt the stranger might be watching her. Or was it all in her head? Rivanah finally took an autorickshaw to her office.

All along she kept an eye around her. Whenever the autorickshaw stopped at any traffic signal she stepped out of the vehicle and looked sharply at other cars, bikes and autorickshaws till at the third traffic signal the auto driver said, '*Madam, aap utarta kaiko rehta hai? Main barabar leke jayega na aapko office.*'

Embarrassed, Rivanah quickly climbed back into the auto. She was convinced the stranger was behind her. But why was he still not making his presence felt? Especially when she needed him the most.

She got off the auto a little before her office. As she walked on the footpath she kept turning back. She thought one particular man was following her. She stopped and let the man pass by. He did. And he didn't care to look at her even once. Any other girl would have been happy to know the man wasn't interested in her. But Rivanah was frustrated. She would have been happy if the man had turned out to be the stranger. She entered her office premises, conscious that her failure to find the stranger was slowly starting to unnerve her. Why was the stranger not approaching her when it was clear that he was still interested in her? Why else would he send the police to save her? And how else would she know how the hell Hiya Chowdhury was linked to her?

Once in her cubicle Rivanah was informed by one of her teammates that their company had invited a psychiatrist for a one-hour pep talk with all its employees on how to bust everyday-life stress and improve productivity at the workplace. Rivanah deliberately skipped the pep talk but went up to the psychiatrist during the lunch break.

'I didn't attend your session,' Rivanah said, apologizing to the psychiatrist. Dr Bineet Ghoshal looked at her and said with a smile, 'It wasn't mandatory. Maybe you already know how to beat stress.'

I *wish!* Rivanah thought and said, 'I have a problem which I don't think will be solved with pep talks.'

'I'm glad you have at least identified and accepted your problem. We can meet in my clinic if you—'

'I don't want to go there.'

The psychiatrist put his plate down on the table, wiped his mouth with a napkin and said, 'Should we take a walk?' Her vulnerable appearance told him she could be an interesting case study.

Soon Rivanah found herself walking with Dr Ghoshal in the smoking zone of her office which was free from the normal office hustle of the lunch hour.

'Tell me,' Dr Ghoshal said.

'I had this person in my life last year.'

'Your boyfriend?'

'No, not boyfriend. You can say a friend. Special friend.' Rivanah chose her words carefully, knowing full well she didn't know the right word to describe her relationship with the stranger.

'He helped me a lot,' she said. 'Like, from pulling me out from a major emotional crisis to help me grow as a person.'

Dr Ghoshal listened intently.

'And now he has disappeared.' Rivanah didn't think the stranger's ways of helping her were any of the doctor's business.

Dr Ghoshal was staring at the floor, listening attentively as he paced up and down slowly with Rivanah by his side. His deep frown told her he was thinking hard. He suddenly stopped. She stopped too.

'And these days whenever you are stressed you miss this person?'

'Exactly.' Rivanah was happy the doctor knew what she was trying to say, without her having to tell him the entire story.

'You miss him because you want him to guide you or de-stress you by giving you solutions to your problems.'

Rivanah thought for a moment and said, 'Maybe.' A pause later she said, 'Not maybe. That is it. I want support and solutions from him.'

'Cinderella complex,' Dr Ghoshal said.

'Huh?'

'You said he rescued you from an emotional crisis, helped you grow as a person, etc., which means in a way he made you depend on him. And now you have developed a complex.'

'Did you say Cinderella complex?'

'Yes. The name is taken from the famous fairy-tale character where the girl needs some external support to stabilize herself. Here too you need him to stabilize your problems. But don't worry . . .'

Dr Ghoshal walked ahead while Rivanah remained where she was, too stunned to move.

Rivanah started to feel disgusted thinking about the stranger. Very cleverly and manipulatively he had pushed her to rely on him and now when she was an emotional loner yearning for him, he wasn't ready to reveal himself but was still keeping an eye like a true sadist.

After Rivanah went back home in the evening, she started searching the whole flat for possible bugs. She even squashed a couple of cockroaches but they were real ones, unlike the ones she had found in her Sai Dham Apartment. Frustrated and emotionally exhausted she cried out aloud, 'What do you want from me, stranger?' There was no answer. 'I want to share things with you. And I also want to know how I'm linked to Hiya. Or was that a sadistic joke of yours?' She hoped the stranger had heard her, somehow. Rivanah waited for a possible response, looking at her phone. There was none. She slowly collapsed on the floor, drew her legs to her chest and started sobbing.

'I loved Ekansh.' She was talking to herself. 'He dumped me. I loved Danny. He isn't bothered about me the way I want him to be. I can't share everything with my parents. I don't have any friends in Mumbai any more. The ones outside are busy with their life. I thought I would have you at least.' She rubbed her eyes, took her phone and once again sent messages to all the numbers she had saved as 'stranger'.

Please come back into my life. I really miss you. I need to talk to you. For God's sake . . .

She kept staring at the messages waiting for them to be delivered. One minute . . . two minutes . . . three minutes . . . she sobbed uncontrollably. A few minutes later she lifted her head and unlocked her phone once. It opened directly to the message screen. There was a small tick against one of the messages. Rivanah immediately called that number. Someone answered after the second ring.

'Hello?' Rivanah said, holding her breath.

Nobody spoke.

'I know you are there so why don't you bloody speak up?'

Still no sound.

'I know I went to the police against you but you didn't leave me with any other option. Hello?'

Some breathing was audible now. Rivanah too paused for some time.

'So you won't talk, huh? You think only you can play games with me? I know I'm still important to you; otherwise you wouldn't have called the police the other night to save me. So here's the deal: I'll wait for an hour. Only one more hour. If you don't call me back I'm going to kill myself. And I'm serious about this,' Rivanah said in one breath and cut the line. Her heart was racing fast as she waited for her phone to ring. He couldn't *not* call.

He will call . . . he will call . . . he will call, Rivanah kept repeating under her breath. One minute became twenty with no call flashing on her phone. And with each passing minute fear ate away at her. What if the stranger didn't call? When the fifty-ninth minute came she found herself perspiring with every second. And then the doorbell rang thrice in a row, just the way Danny rang it. She was slightly taken aback. Rivanah stood up, realizing Danny and Nitya had been out since morning. Somehow she didn't desire any company right now. She wanted to be alone. Rivanah reluctantly went to open the door. As she was unlocking it she turned back when the lights of her flat suddenly went off. She turned back to the front door to see who was there but by then the corridor's light had gone off too. In the pitch-darkness a strong fragrance of Just Different, from Hugo Boss, filled her nostrils. Rivanah knew who it was but before she could call out to him she passed out.

8

Rivanah shifted a bit, trying to open her sleep-laden eyes. She felt something soft touch her skin, a white satin bedsheet, and realized she was lying on her stomach. In a flash she turned and sat up. Her clothes were the same as the ones she was wearing the previous night. She looked around and didn't know where exactly she was. It was a tidy room with everything in its place, the interiors were posh and the ambience was cosy. But there was a haunting silence in the room which scared Rivanah. Looking around she knew she was alone and yet she had a feeling she was not. She turned right to see a small bedside table atop which there was a lamp, a menu and a telephone. The menu card had the name 'The Taj' written on it in bold. Below it was the reception's number. She drew herself closer to the table and picked up the phone. She dialled the reception.

'Good morning. The Taj, reception. How may I help you?' said the light voice of a man.

'Hi, I'm Rivanah Bannerjee. I am speaking from your hotel . . . I guess.'

'Yes, ma'am. You checked in last night. Any problem?'

'Who brought me here?'

'One second, ma'am.' Rivanah waited with bated breath.

'Hello, ma'am.' The receptionist was back on line. 'You were brought in here last night by Mr A.K. Bannerjee.'

For a moment Rivanah thought she was hearing the name for the first time and then realized it was her father's.

'What?'

'Mr A.K. Bannerjee,' the receptionist repeated.

'But he is my father,' she blurted.

'Oh, okay.' The receptionist didn't know what else to say. It didn't matter to him who this guy was. The fact that he had already paid for her room's expenses as well as the breakfast was all that mattered to him.

'Ma'am, we have been instructed to serve you breakfast. Please let me know whenever you are ready. I'd be happy to inform room service on your behalf.'

'How did my father look?'

'Sorry?' The receptionist did have an inkling when she was brought in an unconscious state the previous night that something was wrong. Now he was sure: this girl was mad. Why else would anyone ask what his or her father looked like?

'I mean, what did the person who brought me here look like?' Rivanah rephrased the question. It sounded the same to the receptionist.

'He was tall, with a wheatish complexion, long curly hair and . . .'

'And . . .?'

'I'm sorry but that's all I remember, ma'am.'

'Hmm.' *So it wasn't Baba*, Rivanah thought.

'Should I send the breakfast now?'

'In some time,' Rivanah said and put the phone's receiver down. The last thing she remembered was opening the flat's door. She had threatened the stranger before that. And now she was here. A slight smile appeared on Rivanah's face. *The threat worked!* The stranger didn't want her to kill herself. It only meant he was still interested. And he was interested because she was important. But why here in this hotel room? Another thought dawned on her. Neither her parents nor Danny knew where she was. She looked for her mobile phone but it wasn't there. She picked up the hotel landline once again and dialled the reception.

'Good morning, The Taj reception.'

'I've lost my phone and I urgently need to make a call.'

'Please press zero first followed by the number you want to call,' the receptionist said.

'Thanks.' Rivanah put the receiver down and then picked it up again to dial Danny.

'Hello.' He picked it up pretty late.

'It's me.' She wanted to sound normal but she couldn't.

'Hi.' Danny was cold too. 'How is the seminar going?' he added.

'Seminar?'

'You messaged me last night saying you were going to Pune for a seminar?'

Rivanah couldn't believe it. And yet she believed it. This was nothing compared to what the stranger had done before to her, for her.

'Yes. The seminar is indeed going well.'

There was an awkward silence.

'When will you be back?' Danny asked.

'Soon.'

Both wanted to say 'love you' but neither said it and the call ended with a dry 'see you' instead.

She called her parents next. God knows what the stranger had told them, she thought.

'Mumma!'

'Mini, thank God that you messaged; your baba and I were really worried.'

'Messaged what?'

'That there's some network issue in Mumbai. And you aren't able to call. We tried to call but your phone was unreachable. Is the network all right now?'

'Yes, Mumma, how else do you think I'm calling now?' In a way Rivanah was thankful to the stranger that he did inform her parents else they would have been in Mumbai this morning. She was talking to her mother when the room's bell rang. She said bye quickly and went to open the door. It was room service.

'French breakfast for you, ma'am,' the man in the hotel uniform said, holding a tray. Rivanah moved aside as he entered the room. He went in and put the tray on the centre table. The man went to one side and pressed a button on a wall. The curtains in the room slowly began to draw themselves to a side. And the view that came up left Rivanah spellbound. She could see the Gateway of India at some distance and the bustling crowd around it. She had never seen Mumbai from this point of view.

'Enjoy your breakfast, ma'am.'

Rivanah turned to see the man leave and locked the room's door behind him. She came forward and inspected the tray. It had some fresh fruits in a bowl, a couple of crepes, a croissant and jam and cafe latte in a long glass. The timing of the breakfast couldn't have been better. Rivanah applied some jam on the croissant and took a bite—it was delicious. She was full after having half of it, gazing out the giant window. Picking up the cafe latte, her eyes fell on a tiny pen drive lying below it. She kept her coffee aside and picked it up. On it was written: Mini. She frowned. Did the hotel boy know about it? Or had it been placed here without anyone's knowledge? She looked towards the big LED television in the room. She went and plugged the pen drive in, and in no time she was checking its content using the remote. There was a video there. She played it.

'Oh my God!' she gasped as she watched the video. It showed the badly bruised faces of the triplets. All three looked dazed. And all of them were muttering the same thing: *I'm sorry, Mini.* Rivanah didn't know what to do with it. Precisely then she heard a sound. She listened hard. Somewhere something was . . . ringing. Rivanah paused the video and followed the sound to a corner of the room which had a dressing table and a closet. She opened the closet which was empty except for a small old Nokia phone placed on one of its shelves. She picked it up. A private number was flashing on it. She answered the call.

'Hello,' Rivanah said anxiously.

'Hello, Mini.'

It was the stranger! The voice was deep, solid and piercing.

'Are you the . . .?'

'I'm the one you were seeking so desperately.' This time the voice changed to that of a kid. Rivanah frowned but realized instantly that the person must be using a voice morphing software and was probably calling from a computer.

'This isn't your real voice?'

'Is this your real self?' He sounded like an old man this time. The question made her recollect something: *When was the last time you made a terrible, terrible mistake?* The stranger had asked her this many times.

'What's up with this video?'

'The triplets who tried to take advantage of you the other night. They went scot-free after bribing the police. And the next weekend it was some other girl they tried to hunt. So I hunted them down and did a few things so that they never hunt again.'

A smile shone on Rivanah's face.

'Thanks for helping me the other night'.

'You are welcome, Mini.'

There was silence. Rivanah was happy to connect to the stranger. Perhaps the psychiatrist was right. She indeed was suffering from the Cinderella complex. She took her time to frame her next question and kept it simple.

'Who is Hiya Chowdhury?' she asked.

'If I had to tell you I would have done so by now.'

'So, you want me to know but you don't want to tell me?'

'You are becoming smarter, Mini. I like it.'

A tiny smile appeared on Rivanah's face. After a long time she was feeling calm talking to someone. Only she knew how much she had waited for this.

'So, you are not going to tell me anything about Hiya, right?'

'No.'

'And you won't let me rest too if I don't seek the answer myself?'

'You are not only smarter now but you are getting to know me too.'

The tiny smile stretched into a big one. She would find out how exactly Hiya was linked to her but before that she had other things on her mind.

'I have things to tell you,' she said.

The silence that followed told her that the stranger was listening. She continued, 'I presume you know what's happening between Danny and me. Nitya has come to live with us and—'

'I know.' The stranger cut her short.

'Well, I feel my relationship with Danny is slipping out of our grasp . . . maybe *my* grasp. It makes me feel miserable. I'm losing myself too in the process.'

'You can't hold on to something by questioning it all the time.' The stranger was back to the deep, piercing male voice.

'How can I not question it? From the time Nitya has come into our life, our house, I have almost been compelled to see what I kept myself away from earlier—Danny and Nitya together. Yes, I'm jealous. Maybe I won't admit this in front of Danny or Nitya, but I won't hide it from you. I'm jealous of the closeness they share. Somewhere it makes me feel my connection with Danny is inferior. The exclusivity I thought I enjoyed, I see Danny giving it to Nitya. And I don't like it one bit.'

'We presume that with love comes exclusivity. Since we presume it, we believe it even more strongly. With love comes only one thing: honesty. And honesty is different from loyalty. Most of us never get this difference. Most of us never remain happy in a relationship either.'

'But I'm both loyal and honest.'

'Choose your gods wisely, Mini, for they'll decide how well you fight your demons."

'Meaning?'

'If you were honest then you wouldn't have suffered so much within you. You would have expressed it all to Danny.'

'But if I do that then he would think I'm an insensitive, jealous bitch.'

'What do you have a problem with, Mini? Whether you are an insensitive, jealous bitch or Danny knowing that you are one?'

This time Rivanah was left with no words.

'Am I one?'

The stranger's response was a prolonged silence.

'What should I do?' Rivanah said, concerned. 'I don't want to lose Danny.'

'Go away for a while. Sometimes physical distance throws light on what emotional closeness conveniently eclipses. Whatever he isn't able to see right now perhaps will be clear to him once there's some distance.'

'You mean I should stop living with him?'

'Precisely.'

Rivanah thought hard and said, 'You told me about Ekansh's affair once. So . . . what I mean is . . . could you help me find out if Danny and Nitya are having an affair behind my back? Look, I just want to be sure. It will help me—'

'I can do that for you.'

A wave of relief encompassed her as she said, 'I can't thank you enough.'

'You can thank me by resigning from your job,' the stranger said.

It took a few seconds for Rivanah to understand what she had heard. She said, 'Resign from my job? Are you out of your mind?'

'This isn't your job, Mini.' For the first time he sounded threatening during the call.

'I secured this job during the campus recruitment in my college with my hard work. Whose job is it then, if not mine?'

'Do I need to name her? I thought you were becoming smarter, Mini.'

Rivanah's lips slowly parted with astonishment.

'Who the hell is Hiya Chowdhury? I don't even remember her face,' she said.

'She is the bridge.'

'Why the hell can't you meet me and clarify everything once and for all?'

'If I clarify everything, then the purpose will fail.'

'What's the purpose?'

A few silent seconds later the stranger said, 'Know your worth, Mini.'

9

Rivanah came back to her flat an hour after her talk with the stranger ended. Nitya opened the door, showing no pleasure or displeasure in seeing her. It was only a plain 'Hi' that Rivanah blurted which was reciprocated with equal plainness from Nitya's side. Danny came to the drawing room all dressed up.

'Hi, dear. I have to leave now. See you in the evening.' He kissed her cheek and went out. Nitya had disappeared into the kitchen by then. Rivanah went to the adjacent window and looked down to see Danny drive away from the parking spot below the apartment. He didn't even ask if she had had her breakfast, if she would rest or go to office . . . nothing! Most importantly he didn't even care to know if the seminar had actually happened or not. Had he really started taking her for granted? She could have had an affair and Danny wouldn't know. Worse, he wouldn't inquire. Had things come to such a rotten state or was she thinking too much? Or was it Nitya who was slowly blurring her presence for him? Rivanah felt a thud in her heart. Was the stranger right? Should she distance herself a bit to make herself and the problem of their relationship more visible to Danny? Considering there indeed was a problem and she wasn't exaggerating.

That day, Rivanah searched for her appointment letter in her mail's inbox. She clicked it open and read the contents carefully. It was *her* appointment letter. Tech Sky had come to her college. She had cleared the prelims first and then the HR round. She remembered it clearly, so how could it be Hiya's job? She searched with 'Hiya Chowdhury' in her mail. No mails came up. Clueless, she carried on with her office work. The pressure at office made her forget about the issue for the time being.

When she came back in the evening to her flat she found Nitya alone. She joined her for a cup of ginger tea in the drawing room after freshening up.

'The ginger tea is amazing,' Rivanah said, sipping the tea.

'Thanks.'

'No work today?' Rivanah was being kind to her and trying to strike up a conversation only to unknot whatever she had against Nitya within her. Maybe there was indeed nothing between Danny and Nitya, she thought, and tried hard to believe it.

'There was but I did it over the phone,' Nitya said with eyes fixed on the television.

'How are you feeling now?' Rivanah said, looking at the television where a boring soap was going on.

'You want me to leave the flat soon, don't you?' Nitya said, still not looking at Rivanah. The latter looked at Nitya with a taken-aback expression. She wasn't expecting her to interpret what she said this way. It disturbed her.

'Why would you say such a thing?' Rivanah said, not caring to hide her irritation.

'Because you are jealous of Danny and me, isn't it?' This time Nitya turned to look straight at Rivanah.

'Jealous? Why would I be jealous?' She was, she knew. But she didn't owe a confession to Nitya.

'I would have been. Namrata was.'

'Namrata?'

'Danny's ex-girlfriend.'

Danny did tell her about Namrata but it was in passing and Rivanah didn't remember much.

'Well, I'm not Namrata,' she said. And then added spitefully, 'And yes, I would like to know by when you can leave, if not soon.' She knew she shouldn't have been so rude but Nitya asked for it, she told herself.

'Maybe tomorrow. Or maybe never. Maybe this time you will have to leave,' Nitya said in a casual tone.

But in that casual tone Rivanah could feel a pulsating threat.

'What do you mean?' She put the cup of ginger tea away.

'I don't know whether you have understood till now or not that Danny is not the marrying type. It's not that he won't marry *you*. The fact is he won't marry anyone no matter how close he is to that person. And that way we both are similar. Even I'm not the marrying type.'

'But I'm sure Danny will change for me even if for a second I presume what you said about Danny is right, doesn't matter how much I doubt it otherwise.'

'I have known Danny for the last nine years.'

I knew Ekansh for six years and still I didn't know shit about him. 'I'm sorry, but you still don't know him yet. Moreover, you know him as a best friend and I know him as a boyfriend. There's a difference.' The last part was meant to injure her. The last part was deliberate.

'Why don't we test it?'

'What for?'

'Just to find out who knows Danny better?'

'Is it some kind of competition?'

'Are you getting scared, dear?'

Rivanah and Nitya's eyes remain locked for a few seconds after which the former said, 'Okay, how do we test it?'

'Ask him about marriage. If he agrees to it then great and if not . . .'

'If not?'

'Then you will know you are wasting your time . . . just like Namrata was.'

One thing Rivanah was sure of now: she wasn't wrong about Nitya's vibes. They wouldn't have had this discussion otherwise. She indeed coveted Danny secretly. It was possible she envied the closeness that Danny and Rivanah's relationship had in comparison to hers with her ex. Rivanah went to her room without stretching the talk.

Danny came home late at night. He was hungry. Rivanah had thrown whatever Nitya had cooked for him in the trash can and cooked for him herself. With a fake smile plastered on her face, she listened to Danny rave about how successful his audition was and how much the producer had liked him. There was no interruption from Nitya. In her mind Rivanah was preparing herself. Once Danny switched off the lights in their bedroom, she first closed the door and then came close to sit beside him on the bed.

'You want to say something?' Danny said, looking at her in the dark. She was glad the lights were off. She didn't want to see his reaction but only hear it.

'Let's get married, Danny.' She put it to him simple and straight.

81

There was a momentary silence. Her mind said it was hesitation, while her heart said otherwise. Somewhere in between she died.

'Sure, baby,' Danny mumbled.

For a moment Rivanah wanted to jump up with happiness and then realized Danny could be joking.

'I'm serious,' she said. Danny sat up.

'You can't be.'

'I am.'

'What about your parents?'

'So, are you waiting for them to give a nod to our relationship?'

'Obviously!'

'What "obviously", Danny? You know they won't ever agree to this.'

'Then why are you suddenly so gung-ho about it?'

'You and I love each other. Isn't that a good reason to be gung-ho about it?'

'It is, but why now? Why can't it wait till I get something concrete?'

'So, we will get married right after you secure a movie deal?'

'Of course we will. Why, don't you want to marry me?'

She heaved a sigh of relief. It was only now that Rivanah wanted to see his expression.

'Statue!' she exclaimed. After a long time their love story was experiencing a sunrise. She slowly kissed him all over his face while Danny tried to keep still with a funny expression on his face. She looked at him once, smiled naughtily and then kissed him again; this time harder, biting his nose. She lifted his hands and took his tee off. Lying on his back Danny tried to move but she glared at him.

'No movement, Mr Statue,' she said and pulled the elastic of his knickers, tugging down his briefs. She was excited to see his penis was already hard. She gave him an amused smile as she started blowing him slowly. Suddenly everything seemed back to normal. It wasn't the sex alone but the sense of acute belonging that it brewed in her that excited her the most. As Danny locked his jaws with pleasure, Rivanah tugged her shorts and panties down and rode him. She herself placed his hands on her butt and put hers on his chest. As she started riding him she wondered how Nitya would react if she saw them now. It aroused her even more and she increased her speed. She intentionally moaned with a higher pitch than usual so that Nitya heard them. She collapsed on Danny's chest as both climaxed together.

'Can't you statue me every night?' Danny whispered in her ears. She looked up at him and laughed. As her laughter faded they looked into the other's eyes. They spoke a truth: he was hers. She was his. So what was the problem? She gently placed her head on his chest as he wrapped his arms around her. They went to sleep like that.

Rivanah woke up after some time, took out a post-it slip from the bedside table's drawer and wrote on it: *Surprise, surprise! Danny and I are getting married. You are invited!*

She took the post-it and went to the drawing room. Nitya was sleeping there. She noticed her phone by her side. Rivanah stuck the slip behind Nitya's phone so that she would wake up to it first thing in the morning. And with a victor's smile she went back to her bedroom. Danny was asleep but she wasn't sleepy.

She opened her laptop and logged on to Facebook. She updated: *After a really long time—feeling blessed.* While checking out her friends' updates, an idea struck Rivanah. She checked for Hiya Chowdhury's profile on Facebook. To her surprise she found one. The profile picture was a girl's photo taken from a side angle. Someone she didn't remember. She and Hiya had three mutual friends. All of them were her college batchmates: Sumit, Sonakshi and Ritam. Could they know something about Hiya that she didn't? The rest of the pictures and information was locked. There was no cover photo either. On an impulse she clicked on the Add Friend button before she remembered Hiya was no more. Who would add her? There was no way she could see Hiya's other photographs. Rivanah scrolled down and saw the last timeline post by someone named Argho Chowdhury. The post said: *RIP Hiya di*. She clicked on Argho's profile, which had a close-up of him wearing sunglasses. As Rivanah scrolled down his profile, a particular piece of information caught her eye: Argho's current location. It said Mumbai. And he had updated it exactly the day Rivanah had come to Mumbai a year back. *A coincidence?* Rivanah was wondering when she received a notification which made her break into a cold sweat: *Hiya Chowdhury has accepted your friend request.*

10

Rivanah swallowed the lump in her throat before clicking on the latest notification on her Facebook profile. The next instant she was on Hiya Chowdhury's profile once again. Only this time nothing was locked any more since her friend request had been accepted. Rivanah clicked on the photo section. Except for the profile picture, there was no other photo. It was difficult to make out Hiya's face in the profile picture. She checked that it had been uploaded some time last year. The date didn't have any apparent significance. She checked her friends list. There were a total of fifty friends. Apart from the college batchmates Rivanah knew none. Of course there was Argho Chowdhury as well. She quickly checked her timeline. No posts except for one. And that one made her heart stop for a second. It read: *I'm super excited. Tomorrow my dream company is coming to my college for recruitment. Please pray for me.*

The message had been posted two days before Tech Sky came to their college. And they had recruited only one student from their batch: *Rivanah Banerjee*. She immediately messaged her on Facebook: *Who is this?*

The next minute a 'Seen' appeared beside her message along with the time. *Who could be operating the account? The stranger himself? Then why would he not respond?* Rivanah wondered and waited for a reply. None came. An hour later her eyes started to ache. She pushed her chair back and went to her bed with a clogged mind. She had to think about what was happening but she didn't know where to start. Bouncing off her thoughts from nothing to everything to anything, she finally surrendered to sleep.

Next morning the first thing she did was check for a reply from Hiya Chowdhury's account on Facebook. There was still none. While leaving for her office, she noticed Nitya looking at her. Her face told her that she had read the Post-it. It was Rivanah's way of telling Nitya that not only was she wrong, but she better keep her unwanted and untrue opinion to herself in the future. She closed the door behind her and walked off, feeling happy after a long time.

Once in office Rivanah logged on to her Facebook account from her desktop computer. She went directly to Messages. There was still no reply from Hiya

Chowdhury's account. She clicked on her name and realized it wasn't hyperlinked. It meant either the user had blocked her or had deactivated the account. She quickly copied the URL from her browser, created another Facebook account and pasted the URL on the browser. The profile didn't open. Hiya Chowdhury's profile had been deactivated. *Shit!* Rivanah muttered under her breath. Her gut feeling told her this account would never be activated again. But then why was it active for this long anyway? *Only for me to stumble upon it?* She answered her own query. *That's odd*, she thought. But everything about this whole Hiya Chowdhury mystery was, in one word, odd.

Rivanah kept thinking about it. During lunch the fact struck her that only Argho's comment was visible on Hiya's timeline apart from her status update about the company's arrival in college, which told her it could be a possible clue to something. Or . . . a dreadful thought occurred to her at that moment. Was Argho . . . the stranger himself? *To reach me you have to reach yourself . . . Hiya is a bridge.* Rivanah was astounded at this link. Could it be that she had finally spotted the stranger? She would know only if she met up with Argho Chowdhury.

From the canteen Rivanah went back to her desktop and opened Argho's profile. She was close to clicking on the Add Friend button but stopped. *What if this profile too gets deactivated like Hiya Chowdhury's?* Rivanah instead clicked on the About Me section of Argho's profile. It opened to tell her that he worked as an HR person in a start-up IT firm called Neptune Solutions Technology Pvt. Ltd. Rivanah googled the IT firm's name and went to its official page. She further explored its Contact Us section and came to know the office was in the Mindspace area in Malad West. There were a couple of landline numbers too. She called up and told the lady who answered, 'Hello, I would like to talk to Argho Chowdhury.'

'Certainly, ma'am,' the lady said, but before she could connect to Argho, Rivanah cut the line. She only wanted to know if there was an Argho working there or not.

In the next two minutes she made a decision. The decision gave way to a plan. Rivanah would zero down on Argho and follow him first to see what he was up to, and only if need be, she would introduce herself. The plan was put to execution. She complained to her team lead that she had indigestion and had thrown up three times. The team lead gave her a half-day. She immediately left her office and took an autorickshaw to Malad West. She located the IT firm quite easily. She didn't go inside. If Argho was indeed the stranger then he would know her. In that case, if he saw her, he would either approach her or avoid her. Moreover, how do you enter a company office when you have no appointment or interview? Either way, she didn't want him to notice her just yet. Rivanah once again called the front office landline number of the firm. When the phone was picked up she directly asked if Argho Chowdhury was available.

'Yes, please hold on,' the lady on the other side said.

'Excuse me, but what are the working hours?'

'9 a.m. to 6.30 p.m. Please wait while I get Argho sir on the line.'

Rivanah immediately hung up. Her job was done. Argho was inside at the moment. She looked around and noticed a cafe across the street. She went inside and took a seat from where she could keep an eye on who was going in and coming out. She was sure to identify Argho because she had perused every unlocked picture of his.

At around 6.30 p.m., people started moving out of the building. By then Rivanah had had three cups of coffee. She stood up with her eyes fixed on the exit. She prayed hard that she wouldn't miss Argho because the chances of her missing him were more than those of spotting him in the surge of people. A few more minutes of waiting and then she saw Argho coming out, talking on the phone. He walked to the bus stop and stood there, smoking a cigarette while continuing to talk on the phone. Rivanah prayed he didn't have a bike or any vehicle; otherwise following him would be tough. Soon, he dropped the cigarette, stamped it out and climbed into an auto which had slowed down by the stop. Rivanah quickly took an autorickshaw herself and asked the driver to follow Argho's auto. The driver did exactly as he was asked to. It was only when the auto reached Andheri West station that she saw Argho getting down. She too got down, paid the auto driver and started following him on foot.

As Argho took the West–East bridge, she too did the same. There was a good hundred metres between them. All she wanted to know was where he lived. Once she knew that she could find out a lot more and most importantly if he indeed was the stranger.

Suddenly Argho kneeled down. Rivanah turned around and in a flash had her phone against her ear as if she was talking to someone. Her heart was in her mouth. She could feel her body was trembling slightly with tension. From the corner of her eyes she noticed Argho was only tying his shoelace. She relaxed. And started following him once he started walking again. He crossed the bridge and finally took the direction for the metro. For Rivanah it was the first time at the Mumbai Metro. Looking around cluelessly, she tried to do whatever Argho was doing. She took the escalator to move up like he did, went a floor above the ground level, walked straight, took a turn and saw Argho in the ticket queue. She tried but couldn't hear which station he was heading to. She took another queue and as she reached the ticket window, she turned to see him pass through the security check.

'Which is the last stop?' she asked the girl behind the ticket counter.

'Versova at one end and Ghatkopar on the other,' the girl said indifferently.

Rivanah knew Versova was towards Andheri West where he could have taken the auto itself which meant he was definitely going somewhere towards . . .

'Ghatkopar,' she said. She got the ticket and without caring to take her change rushed towards the security check, after which she proceeded to the automated gate where she touched her ticket on the top of the machine for the gate to open. She passed through it looking ahead. Argho was climbing the stairs for the Ghatkopar-bound train. Rivanah almost scampered towards it, waited by the stairs for a moment and then climbed up. She was gasping for air when she reached the platform. A casual glance to her left told her he was standing amidst other men at a distance. The metro arrived in the next minute.

Men were blocking the door through which Argho had entered. Rivanah entered two compartments ahead but walked through the vestibule and reached the same compartment as Argho's. She hid herself behind a tall man in a way so that she could keep an eye on Argho without him noticing her. One after another, stations went by and Argho finally moved out at Saki Naka station. So did she. Following him, she reached the exit. He was waiting for the elevator with a few others. Rivanah waited at a distance, knowing she couldn't risk going close to him just yet. As he entered the elevator with the others and the door closed, she hurried towards the escalator. But to her frustration she realized the escalator was going up. The only way she could go down was by the elevator. She waited with some others hoping Argho didn't go out of sight. She rushed into the elevator the moment it arrived again. In a few seconds it took her to the street below. As she came out on the street outside another set of people rushed into the elevator. She looked around. There was no sign of Argho.

Damn!

'Madam, is it yours?' said someone who was about to enter the elevator.

It was a white piece of cloth with something embroidered in black. It was not hers. But she knew it was definitely meant for her. She stretched her hand and took it from the person. The elevator door closed. She read the message on it:

I'll be glad if you get to me. But once you do, you shall destroy yourself forever, Mini. The choice is yours.

For a moment she couldn't breathe. The passive-aggressive threat that the message communicated hit Rivanah hard. She could feel a certain fear escalate right from within her guts. She took out a bottle of water from her bag and drank from it. There were two things hovering on her mind right then: one, she had finally zeroed in on the stranger; two, the cloth message also told her that Argho knew she would come after him. Once again she looked around but knew she had lost him for the time being. Or maybe he was looking at her from somewhere. She checked her phone for some message, perhaps from an unknown number. There was nothing. Disappointed, she took the escalator up and went back to Andheri first and then home.

She opened the flat with her spare keys. The silence told her there was nobody inside. She switched on the lights and was about to take off her sandals when her phone buzzed with five messages. For a second she thought it could be the stranger—Argho—messaging her. She checked the messages. A couple of audio messages from Nitya. She played the last one. Nitya's voice said, *Congrats indeed, Rivanah.* She played the second-last audio message and heard Danny's voice. What he said stole the air out of her lungs.

Rivanah was sitting on one of the two La-Z Boy chairs in the drawing room, trying hard not to think about the messages Nitya had sent, and yet she could still hear Danny's voice from the audio. Her body temperature had risen a bit and she could feel anger gushing within her like a fierce wind. And with the anger there was a certain instability that she could feel that wasn't letting her think straight. The doorbell rang after a good one and a half hour. Nitya's laughter was audible and so was Danny's. Rivanah got up and opened the door. The way she stalked back to the chair without even caring to look at them piqued both Danny and Nitya. Danny immediately sensed something was wrong.

'What happened?' he asked.

Rivanah, with a straight face, glanced at Nitya once. There was a slight hint of amusement on Nitya's face which told Rivanah she knew exactly what had happened. Rivanah gave the phone to Danny. He took it and played the audio file. He knew exactly when this had been recorded. In the morning after Rivanah had left for her office, when Danny was having his green tea with Nitya sitting on the couch in the room he was in right now.

'*I don't know what to do really!*' Danny's voice from the audio reverberated in the quietness of the room.

'*Why, what happened?*' It was Nitya's voice.

'*Whenever Rivanah talks to me about marriage it just gets to me. I want to be with her, but I don't know why she keeps harping about marriage all the time. As if we are in a relationship only to get married. Why does she do it?*'

'*Did you tell her that?*'

'*You think she'll understand? I always have to lie to her face that we'll get married, but the whole idea of marriage screws my mind up. I love Rivanah. But this one thing about her just irritates me.*'

'*So you don't want to marry Rivanah?*'

'*No, I don't want to. I mean I don't understand the need for marriage.*'

The audio was over. Danny didn't know where to look. He had said whatever he felt in the audio and that made him feel all the more guilty. He couldn't look at Rivanah. He turned to Nitya instead.

'What's this?' he asked.

'Rivanah said you would marry her. I said you won't. A little game between us which she thought she won last

97

night.' She glanced at Rivanah and said, 'You now know who won, don't you?'

Rivanah didn't look at Nitya. Looking straight at Danny, she said, 'Why couldn't you tell me this?'

'I wanted to, but I was scared that you wouldn't understand me.'

For a moment everything about Danny seemed like Ekansh to her.

'What else didn't you tell me, Danny, safely presuming that I wouldn't understand it?'

'Trust me; I haven't hidden anything from you.'

'*Trust?* If you don't already realized it by now, then let me tell you: this "trust" becomes a funny thing once you realize the person can lie to you.'

'I didn't lie to you, Rivanah. I just—'

'Yes, you lied. And don't you try to tell yourself or me otherwise. When I asked you last night you said you were more than okay with marrying me. Why can't you men just be straight about a few things?' Rivanah turned and was about to dash towards the front door when Danny grabbed her hand.

'Let go of me, Danny.' She was fuming.

'I'm sorry, Rivanah. It's not what you think. I can explain. I love you,' Danny pleaded.

Rivanah shot a glance at him. *I can explain* . . . the same words Ekansh had once used. When you are a tourist every place is exciting but as a native every place is the same, monotonous. The first day she had seen Danny in a towel she had been a tourist. Now she was a native. She knew him better. A bud of an ironic smile stretched her lips but before it could flower further, Rivanah checked it.

'I understand, Danny, and that's why you don't have to explain anything.' She shook his hand off and added, 'Just message me when you won't be home; I will come and clear out my stuff.'

'What? Where will you stay?'

'Never mind.' Rivanah spoke softly this time. She stepped out and shut the door behind her. For some time Danny stood still, looking tense and anxious. Then he looked at Nitya who was now sitting in the La-Z Boy where Rivanah had been a moment back.

'It wasn't just a game, was it, Nitya? You wanted her place, right?' Danny said.

'No, Danny. What are you saying?' She stood up and came to him and, putting her hands around his neck, said, 'I wanted *my* place, not hers. Don't you get it? You and I were always supposed to be together. It was foolish of me to get into another relationship, but, after the break-up, I realized if there is someone who will always understand me, that's you, Danny. That's you!'

'Before recording that message, didn't you think that I actually loved Rivanah?' he said, removing her hands from around his neck and moving away.

'I did, but then Rivanah and you don't have a future. You said so yourself in the audio. You both want different things from the relationship. But you and I want the same thing. I will never ask you to marry me. *Never ever.*' She tried to come close again but Danny stopped her.

'I want you to go back to your flat, Nitya.'

'Danny . . . listen . . . you are not able to—'

'Right now, Nitya, before I forget you were my best friend once.'

Nitya staggered. Danny went into the bedroom and locked himself in.

From her flat in Andheri Rivanah took an autorickshaw straight to Meghna's place in Goregaon East. She had called her to check if she was at home. She was. Rivanah kept rubbing her tears off but they didn't seem to stop. She knew there were things that even she had never told Danny about, and she was blaming him for the same emotional crime that she too had committed. And yet she couldn't bring herself to forgive him. She wouldn't be able to go back to the flat. That was final. Would she go back to Danny? She wasn't ready to answer this because she didn't yet know if it was even a question.

Meghna opened the door for Rivanah. She was meeting her after nine or ten months. After she had left her place Rivanah had gone to live on her own for the first time. So much had happened since then, she thought, and hugged Meghna.

'You remember your Meghna di only when you need something, no? Where were you all these months?'

'I'm so sorry, Di. I always wanted to call up and meet but—'

'But time flies, I keep busy and all that. It is okay; even I give the same excuse to everyone.'

They laughed as Meghna welcomed Rivanah into the drawing room. Meghna excused herself to finish some office work on the laptop while Rivanah relaxed on the sofa-cum-bed in the drawing room. The same one on which she had had the most amazing phone sex of her life with Ekansh. Where did that time go? What happened to that Rivanah who was so happy with life? *Life kills you more acutely than death*, she thought and tried to close her eyes to sleep when the doorbell rang.

'Mini, will you please see who it is?' Meghna shouted from the bedroom.

'Sure, Di.' Rivanah stood up and went to open the door. It was a young guy with spiked hair, red tee, royal-blue denims and Converse shoes. His ears were plugged with white earphones. He took out the earplug on seeing Rivanah.

'Yes?' she said.

'Umm . . . This is where Meghna lives, right?'

His accent told her he was from the North-east. 'Yes,' Rivanah said without registering why such a young guy would refer to Meghna by name.

'Then who are you?' he asked.

'I'm Rivanah, her cousin. But who are you?'

'I stay here.'

'Excuse me?'

'I live with Meghna.'

Before Rivanah knew it, her jaw had already dropped. Meghna was standing behind her by then.

'Come in, Riju,' Meghna said. Rivanah slowly moved out of the way as Riju came in.

'Freshen up. I will make tea for you,' Meghna said. Riju nodded and disappeared inside. Meghna closed the door and said, 'Aadil and I are divorced now. Nobody at home knows. And I hope you will keep it to yourself,' and went to stand by the window in the drawing room. She knew Rivanah would come up to her.

'Aadil da and you are divorced?!'

'We tried our best but it didn't work out.' There was silence, after which Meghna continued, 'Or maybe we didn't really try our best because we knew that if we did we would have saved our relationship but neither of us wanted that. A saved relationship is no relationship, after all.'

'I don't understand it, Meghna di. Why would you not want the relationship for which you guys fought your families?'

'I don't want to go into it again, Mini. I only know that, with Riju, I'm trying to make a start. A fresh start at life.'

'But he looks like a—'

'He is a second-year college student. Thirteen years younger.'

'And you are okay with it?'

Meghna looked at Rivanah and said, 'Aadil was someone I fell in love with. Wasn't I okay with him? I have stopped bracketing relationships with good, bad, right, wrong, okay, not okay.'

The breeze coming in through the window ruffled Rivanah's hair. She brushed a few strands of hair away from her face, still unable to process what she had heard.

'I will prepare tea for all of us,' Meghna said and went to the kitchen.

Rivanah had nothing against Riju but she couldn't bring herself to talk to him properly for the rest of the night. When they sat together for dinner she could see Meghna was happy with Riju: the way they talked, touching each other at the slightest of excuses, holding hands while eating, and the way Meghna took care of him was proof of their love. And yet all of it disturbed Rivanah. She knew whatever Meghna was doing was because of lack of an option. Age wasn't the factor but the way Meghna was trying to fit into the relationship that she said she shared with Riju didn't seem organic to Rivanah. Would she too end up like this? She wanted to call Danny and tell him that she forgave him and that marriage wasn't necessary and that they should start afresh. But then she realized she was a human being after all. And with human beings everything has a ramification. Her coming to this flat would have a ramification as much as her going back to Danny now would. What if he started taking for her granted all the more?

Rivanah went to the washbasin and splashed some water on her face. Her mind was akin to a traffic signal where no thought vehicle was following any rule. And they caused one messy traffic jam. As she rested on the sofa-cum-bed and tried to sleep, she thought about what would have happened had Ekansh not cheated on her. By now she would have been living with him, making more and more memories with him. He must have applied for an MBA but before that she would have made sure they were engaged. Two more years and they would have gotten married, moved abroad to some beautiful place and spent their life happily together. But it didn't happen. What happened was that Ekansh turned out to be a dog. It taught her a simple truth: even if you love someone truly, things could still turn out badly. She turned on the sofa-cum-bed trying to force herself to sleep when she heard the doorbell. She checked her mobile phone lying beside her. It was 11.30 p.m. She remained still, hoping Meghna or Riju would come out and open the door. Then she recollected the two had gone out for a late-night movie after dinner. They had asked her but she had cited a false headache. The doorbell rang again. Rivanah got up and went to the door. She looked through the peephole. And she had her heart in her mouth.

'Hiya!' she mumbled to herself with fear churning her guts.

12

Rivanah pulled herself back from the door, her heart racing and hands trembling. Her knees felt weak. This couldn't be possible. Hiya Chowdhury was *dead*. People whom she trusted had confirmed this for her. The doorbell rang again. *This is not even a dream*, Rivanah thought, and once again looked through the peephole. Hiya Chowdhury was still standing there wearing a salwar suit.

'Who is this?' Rivanah asked aloud. Her voice had a scared trill to it.

'Didi, it is me . . . Swati.'

A slight frown appeared on Rivanah's forehead and she immediately opened the door.

'Swati?' she said, looking at the girl whose picture she had seen as Hiya Chowdhury's profile picture. Though the picture on Facebook was not very clear, she could tell it was her picture. A closer look and she knew who this Swati was. The last time she had seen her, Swati had been in a dishevelled and bruised state in a municipal hospital in Borivali. Swati had been gang-raped near Aarey Colony. And Rivanah was instrumental in putting those gang rapists behind bars.

'What are you doing here?' Rivanah asked. This was the first time she was actually talking to her.

'My mother asked me to thank you for what you did and give you a hug,' Swati spoke in Hindi but with a heavy Marathi accent.

'You came to thank me at this hour? And how did you know I live here?' Rivanah couldn't hide her surprise.

'I know it is odd, but my mother said a lady told her that this is when you need a hug the most. She gave her your address too. You have done so much for me. A hug at this hour is the least I could do.'

A *lady* . . . Rivanah didn't waste a second trying to figure out who this lady could be. Someone the stranger must have tipped to approach Swati's mother. By now she knew it was useless to go to her and inquire about the stranger.

'Whatever it is that is bothering you, Didi, will be over soon,' Swati said and hugged her.

At least there was someone in this whole world who knew when she craved a shoulder to cry, a hug to dissolve herself in, Rivanah thought, and hugged Swati back tightly. In no time her eyes were wet. She felt like she was emptying herself. As if those tears were words which she was sharing with Swati but in reality were intended for Danny. She could feel Swati's hand caressing her back as if to tell her: cry, if that's what you think will help, then do cry. After some time Rivanah let go of Swati.

'I shall forever be indebted to you,' Swati said before taking her leave. Rivanah was about to close the door when Swati turned back.

'I forgot. Aayi asked me to give you this. The lady gave this to her.' Swati took out a piece of white cloth from her shabby sling bag and gave it to Rivanah. She took it in her hand. By then she knew what it could be. She read the message embroidered in black: *There's a belief according to which the world of the dead and the world of sleep are connected.*

Rivanah swallowed a lump reading it. *World of the dead . . . Hiya . . . world of sleep . . . the nightmare?*

'And this too,' Swati said, giving her another piece of white cloth.

Resign from your job ASAP.

Rivanah was momentarily lost in thoughts when she heard Swati say, 'If you could help me fight such a terrible crisis, I am sure you shall fight yours too. All will be well. Bye for now, Didi.' Rivanah smiled at her before closing the door and wondered what Swati's picture was doing in Hiya's profile. Moreover, Hiya was her batchmate in college. Then why the hell couldn't she remember her face though she remembered her laughter? Till she saw her profile picture on Facebook she thought she had a vague image of her in her mind. The kind which clears up the moment the person or her photograph comes in front of you. But the truth was she didn't remember Hiya Chowdhury at all. And the stranger was taking advantage of it. But why would Argho comment on a fake Hiya's profile? The clouds of confusion hovered in the sky of her mind. There were too many questions and none with any lead to a solid answer. Well, there was one lead. The stranger . . .

The doorbell rang again. It was Meghna and Riju. He had his arm around her shoulder while she had hers around his waist. Something about it made Rivanah abhor them. Why was she being so judgemental about them? Was it because Meghna had found happiness with a guy much younger than her or was it because she hadn't been able to find that happiness with Danny?

'Hey, Rivanah, what's up?' Riju said.

'Still awake?' Meghna said.

'I was about to sleep,' Rivanah said and went to the sofa-cum-bed. Riju and Meghna locked the door and went to the bedroom.

Lying alone on the bed, Rivanah could see the moon outside. She wondered why the stranger wasn't telling her who Hiya Chowdhury was. Why was he playing this game with her? Then she realized the stranger was all about games to begin with. She couldn't resign from her job just like that. It was her identity, the only alternative where she could afford to immerse herself and forget other troubles. Every time she ran from something, it was work that came to her rescue. How could she simply resign? How would she sustain herself? What if she didn't get another job immediately? And then Rivanah suddenly sat up. Something struck her. The stranger had asked her one thing repeatedly: *What is the most important thing in your life?* And she had time and again told him it was Danny. But only now she knew the answer. It was her job that was most important.

She immediately wrote a message for the stranger on her phone and sent it to all the phone numbers she had saved with her.

I need to talk.

A minute later only one of them showed a delivery tick. And right after that her phone rang, flashing a private number.

'Hello, Mini.' It was a man's voice.

'I finally have an answer to your question.'

'I'm listening.'

'You asked me what the most important thing in my life was, right? It is my job. I can't leave it. I can't resign else my life shall collapse.'

'I know.'

'You do? If you know then why are you asking me to resign?'

'So that your life collapses.'

'I want to be really clear with you. I have nothing—absolutely nothing—to do with Hiya Chowdhury. In fact I'm sure you are the one who put Swati's picture on Hiya's profile. This proves I don't even remember her. Then how can you expect me to do away with the most important thing of my life for her?'

'It's not for her. It is for you. You have to resign for your own sake.'

'You know what that would mean? What if I don't get another job?'

'We presume a lot by merely looking at a road. But presumptions limit us, limit our life. You have to walk the road to really know what it has to offer.'

'What if the thing this road has to offer is a big nothing?'

'If you walk a road well, then it will at least offer one basic thing.'

'What's that?'

'You will know your worth a little more, Mini. Every road is an opportunity to know yourself . . . bit by bit. Tougher the road, bigger the bit.'

Rivanah took her time to frame her next question. Should she ask the stranger if it was Argho Chowdhury on the other side? He must know by now that she had been following him, so what was the harm? But what if he didn't know she was following him? Just what if . . . ?

'I need time to think,' she said.

'Think. And think fast. Maybe this road has to offer you something which you are eager to reach.'

'And that is?'

'Me.' And the line went dead.

Dammit! Rivanah thought. She was sure she wouldn't resign but this last bit from the stranger was just the teaser she could have done without. *Oh no, I can't resign just like that.* Her mind was quite numb. She wanted to know how Hiya Chowdhury was linked to her but she couldn't find a way to do so. She wanted to know who the stranger was and now it seemed she had a chance. But it wasn't a mere chance. Resigning from her job sounded more like a price. The stranger had told her before that the job wasn't hers. That was absurd. In fact everything about the stranger was absurd. With sleep being a far cry, she turned over when she heard a moan. Suddenly it went up several decibels. Meghna was moaning out Riju's name. Rivanah shut her ears with both her hands and then after a moment she released her hands only to hear Riju's groan this time. The moans and groans reminded her of too many things and too abruptly: of Ekansh and her, of Danny and her, of Nitya and Danny, of Aadil and Meghna, of everything she didn't want to be reminded of. She rushed for her earphones, put them on and played a random song on her phone. She finally relaxed. Earlier it was Meghna–Aadil's fights which drove her out of the flat and now it was even more irksome. She knew she would have to look for a flat for herself. She checked her phone. There were no messages from Danny. Not a single one. She hadn't messaged him either. So, going back to his flat was not even an option right now. The song she was listening to paused as her phone's screen flashed a private number. She took the call.

'What is it, Mini: yes or no?'

'I'm sorry; I can't resign. And you don't have to tell me anything about Danny and Nitya either,' she said. 'It is—'

'Yes or no?'

'No!'

There was a momentary silence.

'Just to remind you, Mini, every yes or no has . . . consequences.' The stranger cut the line.

13

When the stranger said 'consequences', Rivanah knew it wasn't a joke. It scared her but you don't resign from your job because you are scared of someone whom you have no idea about. More than the stranger this time, she was afraid of the one word the stranger had used: *consequences*. She had had enough of 'consequences' in her life. And she was tired of them. Falling in love with Ekansh had consequences, splitting up with him had consequences, choosing Danny, now staying away from him . . . staying with parents made her meek; living alone made her aware. Life is all about consequences and how you deal with them because Rivanah by now had understood nobody could run away from them. She would have thought more about this if her phone hadn't buzzed with a WhatsApp message just then:

How are you?

It was Danny. He had finally found time to message her.

Good, she wrote back.

The ticks turned blue telling her Danny had read the message. But no reply came. She typed: *And you?* She sent it.

Good. The reply was instant this time.

Hmm.

Hmm.

It was their first official cold war where ego was the deciding factor. With this particular set of messages, she knew, their relationship had entered a new phase; whether it was backward or forward she had no clue. She stared at the WhatsApp message for some time. Danny was online and so was she. But neither communicated. On an impulse she tapped on the phone and it went back to the home screen. Suddenly furious, she switched off her data network and shut her eyes.

The next morning Rivanah left for work before Meghna and Riju had opened their bedroom door. The first thing she did was log on to Facebook to search for flats. Unlike a year ago, now she knew exactly how to talk and negotiate with dealers. She was happy with one particular flat in Goregaon East itself. The dealer had told her the place would be shared by only one more girl. It was a 2 BHK where they would have a room each for themselves as well as a drawing room. Her share was to be twenty-five thousand rupees a month but she managed to bring it down to twenty-two a month. She told the dealer she would be there in the evening after office to check out the place and finalize it if she liked it.

'Hey, Rivanah, did you see this?' It was her team lead Sridhar. Before she could turn and look at him, Sridhar leaned to show her something on her desktop. Though Sridhar had this indecent habit of gaping at her breasts while talking, never before had he come this close to her. His face was too close for Rivanah to be comfortable. She tried to push her chair back but found Sridhar's leg blocking it. He was showing her some Facebook video he could have easily asked her to see from his seat. Why this sudden inclination to come close? 'I'll just be back from the washroom,' Rivanah lied, excusing herself before he could come any closer. Sridhar moved his leg from behind her chair and she pushed it to stand up.

She turned to look at Sridhar who was gaping at her. Till then a mere eye-lock always made him look somewhere else but this time it was Rivanah who looked away.

Right through the day Rivanah caught Sridhar looking at her in a manner she couldn't decipher. It was as if he wanted her to say something. She kept wondering what it was the whole day in the office. After work, Rivanah went to see the apartment in Goregaon. It was on the twelfth floor. The view of the distant hills from the bedroom window made her waste no more time. She told the dealer she would complete all formalities the next day and move in the day after.

'That will be great, madam.' The dealer was happy to have sealed the deal in a day.

'But do you have any idea who will stay with me in the flat?' she asked.

'Not yet.'

'I don't want any weird girl as my roomie,' Rivanah said, remembering Asha from her previous flat. And at the same moment she missed Ishita too. It had been some time since they had had a talk. She made a mental note to contact her soon as she heard the dealer say, 'The other room is still not occupied. And don't worry. You can ask anyone. My record is clean as far as tenants are concerned. No weird people ever.'

Rivanah flashed a plastic smile and said, 'See you tomorrow morning at the registrar's office.'

That night when Rivanah told Meghna about the shift she said, 'Let me know if you need my help.'

'Sure, Di,' Rivanah said, hoping she wouldn't need any such help. Meghna had started to remind Rivanah of what she could pretty well become in the near future. And she didn't like it one bit. Severing herself from Meghna was her priority.

The next morning Rivanah took her luggage to the registrar's office where an eleven-month contract was drawn between the landlord and her, after which she gave the landlord eleven post-dated cheques, went straight to the furnished flat with the keys, put her luggage there, and immediately left for office.

In the office Sridhar yet again kept looking at her expectantly. And during lunch he WhatsApped her: *I'm okay with it.* What was he okay with? Rivanah had no clue. She was about to ask him when someone cleared his throat and asked, 'Are you Rivanah Bannerjee from Sridhar's team?'

She looked up to see a middle-aged man with a slight paunch and a receding hairline looking down at her. His ID was hanging from his neck. She read his name in a flash: Bitan Dey.

'Yes, that's me.'

'Hi, I'm sure you don't know me. I just wanted to tell you that it's okay with me. We can meet after office if you are free. See you.' And he walked off.

It's okay with me—the phrase struck Rivanah hard. Something was wrong. She immediately WhatsApped Sridhar back: *What are you okay with?*

Whatever you wrote in the email, Sridhar replied.

Which email? Rivanah's heart was already racing. She was expecting a WhatsApp reply but Sridhar called her instead.

'The email you sent me a couple of nights ago.'

'But I didn't send any email to you.'

'Come on, Rivanah. It was from your office ID. You don't have to feel shy. It's okay with me.'

Knowing fully well who had sent that mail, Rivanah was disgusted.

'I want to read the email. I'm coming to your desk,' she told Sridhar and cut the line. Before she went to Sridhar, she quickly went to her desktop and checked her Sent Items folder in her office mail account. There was no email from her side to Sridhar or Bitan—by now she had guessed why he had approached her. She dashed to Sridhar's cubicle. The latter was waiting for her with his email open on his desktop.

'Now don't tell me it's not you. See, it has come from your official email ID. Dated day before yesterday; the time was 7.30 p.m.'

Feeling a knot in her stomach she went close to the desktop computer and read the email that she had supposedly sent Sridhar:

Hi Sri,

I have a confession to make. I've started having this thing for you, like a wild animal has for a forest. Will you let me explore the forest?

XOXO

Rivanah

The first thing she did was delete the mail.

'What are you doing?' Sridhar said, trying to push her away but by then she had deleted it from the Recycle Bin as well.

'Why did you do that?' Sridhar looked at her, clueless.

'My office mail was hacked. I never sent this email,' Rivanah said.

Sridhar looked at her for some time and knew she was telling the truth. The email was too good to be true.

'Hmm. You did the right thing by deleting it. But we must catch whoever executed this vulgar joke. I'll register a complaint with the HR.'

'I know who did it,' Rivanah said in one breath.

'You do? Who is it?' Sridhar sounded amazed.

'I don't know the person yet.'

Sridhar frowned and said, 'You know who did it but you don't know the person yet?'

'Never mind. You can complain if you want to, but I don't think it is going to help.' Rivanah turned and slowly walked back to her cubicle, leaving a confused Sridhar behind.

Every yes or no has consequences, the stranger had told her.

In the evening, when Rivanah opened the door to her new flat and stepped in, a whiff of something familiar stopped her dead in her tracks. It was the smell of Just Different from Hugo Boss. The next instant she groped frantically for the switchboard, realizing the obvious: the stranger was in the room; but none of the switches were working. Her first instinct was to run but the stranger's voice stopped her.

'Chill, Mini. I won't harm you,' the stranger said. It was a male voice not matching with any of the ones she had heard till now. Though the voice was slightly mechanical, she could sense he was in the room, only a few feet away from her perhaps.

'Just close the door.'

Rivanah took her time but eventually closed the door to let the darkness engulf the room and her totally.

'You hacked into my office email,' she said, knowing that was obvious. And also knowing how much her voice trembled with fear. Add to it her temporary blindness.

'I could have done worse. You know that.'

'Can you, for God's sake, tell me whether you are a friend or a foe?' Rivanah slowly pushed herself against one of the walls in the room, feeling slightly claustrophobic in the darkness.

'If I was a friend then I wouldn't have hacked your email.'

'Exactly!'

'But if I was a foe I would have sent Sridhar the video I have of you. You know which video I'm talking about, right, Mini?'

121

Rivanah knew it was the same video that he had made when he attacked her in the flat, tearing her clothes off and tying her up.

'Then what are you?' she gasped.

'I'm neither a friend nor a foe. I'm what you want me to be.'

There was silence. Rivanah could feel her throat drying up as she said, 'What if I still don't resign?'

'People in your office will get more emails. Maybe this time with a video attachment.'

Exactly what she had feared a moment back, Rivanah thought as she swallowed a lump.

'This is blackmail,' she mumbled.

'This is me for you.'

A moment later Rivanah said meekly, 'Will you actually send that video out?'

'Don't you try me on this, Mini.'

Rivanah knew the stranger had made her helpless once again. She would have to resign. She would have to let go of the most important thing in her life. Her job. Her identity. A symbol of her independence. And who knows when she would get another job? What if she did and had to return to Kolkata? No, she couldn't just resign. The dormant rebel in her suddenly woke up. The stranger was only few feet away. If she rushed at him while screaming, he could probably be caught.

Yes, he could be caught! And in all probability, it was Argho Chowdhury standing somewhere in the darkness around. On an impulse Rivanah sprang forward without really knowing where the stranger was in the room. She hit a centre table and fell to the floor shrieking out in pain. The lights came on. She turned to look all around the room and at a corner by the window she saw a mobile phone and a tiny speaker attached to it. Her leg throbbing, she almost crawled to the phone. She picked it up only to notice the call was still on.

'Exactly by noon tomorrow you should resign.'

14

Rivanah went to office an hour later than usual. From early in the morning she kept looking at her watch every minute. And with every second she only had one question in her mind: would she actually resign?

The protocol for resignation at her company was simple: anyone wishing to resign had to log on to their internal company portal, log in with one's unique credentials and then click on the Resign button. The employee could revoke it only within twenty-four hours after he or she clicked on the Resign button. She kept staring at the button but couldn't summon enough courage to click on it. Yet. At 11.30 a.m., she messaged all the numbers she had of the stranger.

Can we please do without my resignation?

The next second came a reply from one of the numbers:

Sure, we can.

For a moment Rivanah couldn't believe her eyes. She relaxed, gulping down some water from the bottle on her desk. She finally started her work for the day. Sometime later she got a message from another number which too she had saved in the stranger's name.

But whatever we do . . . has consequences, Mini.

Rivanah glanced at the watch. It was 12.01 p.m. *Past noon!* She looked around to see if she could spot something amiss. *The stranger won't circulate the video. He may say whatever he wants to but he isn't her foe*, she thought. It was precisely then she saw Sridhar walking towards her. Had the stranger forwarded him the video? *Damn,* she muttered under her breath, feeling her throat go dry.

'What's up, Rivanah?' Sridhar inquired.

Rivanah stood up from her chair.

'Why did you resign?' he said.

'What?!'

Rivanah turned in a flash and logged on to the company portal as quickly as she could. As the page loaded, her phone flashed a private number. The page loaded and she noticed her Resign button actually read Revoke which meant someone had already clicked on the Resign button. She immediately was in two minds whether to pick the call up or not. Slowly she answered her phone while taking the mouse to the Revoke button.

'*You click the Revoke button; I'll click the Send button on the email with the video attachment.*'

The line was cut.

'Now don't tell me someone hacked the system and resigned on your behalf,' Sridhar said, expecting Rivanah to come up with a valid explanation.

A few seconds later, Rivanah removed the cursor from the Revoke button and looked at Sridhar guiltily. The latter shrugged.

'No, it wasn't hacked. I've actually resigned.'

'What? Why?'

'I don't know. I'm sorry. Please excuse me.' Rivanah stumbled to the washroom like a ghost and, locking herself in one of the toilets, cried her heart out. Her notice period would begin soon: a total of thirty days. After which she would have to stop coming to office. What would she do after that period?

When she went back to her cubicle, two of her teammates told her the same thing: *This is your worst decision, Rivanah.* Sometime later, another teammate came to her and said, 'I know you must be joining another company, otherwise who resigns just like that? Could you please forward my CV there too? I won't tell anyone here.'

'I'm not joining anywhere else.'

The teammate stared at her and then went away, probably sensing something was wrong with her, and acting as if that something could well be infectious.

Rivanah knew she would soon have to find another job for herself or else it would be difficult for her to survive in Mumbai. And this thought gave way to another thought which felt like a stab: did the stranger want her to leave Mumbai? She sent a message—*I want to talk*—to all the numbers she had of the stranger. But didn't care to check if the message was delivered or not. Her mind was trying to crack the reason behind why the stranger would want to push her out of Mumbai. And where to? Kolkata? Or . . . wherever Hiya Chowdhury's family was?

She got a call from a private number. She took the phone and moved out into the smoking zone where there were only a few people. Once there she answered the call.

'Hello, Mini.'

'Why do you keep giving me such pain?' she asked.

'Let me tell you an amazing thing about pain.' The stranger spoke in a woman's voice this time. 'You give it; you'll get it.'

'How have I given pain to anyone?'

There was silence.

'Okay, now that you have made me resign I want that video of mine. I can't allow this blackmail to continue. Or else I'll be forced to involve Inspector Kamble once again.'

'It was you who said you will kill yourself if I don't come back. It's not good to complain about the chicken you hatched yourself.'

'Every time I start to believe you are a dream, you push me to believe that you are a nightmare. Why?'

'I'm neither your dream nor your nightmare, Mini. I'm what you want me to be.' With this the line went dead.

Rivanah realized it was useless, simply useless, to talk with the stranger about what his intention was. The sooner she reached the truth behind Hiya Chowdhury, the quicker she would be able to decipher what the stranger was all about. But how could she know the truth about a person she remembered nothing about? Not even how she looked. And Hiya Chowdhury was supposed to be her batchmate in college. Or so she had been told.

15

Rivanah came straight to her flat after office. Without caring to switch on the lights, she slumped down on the bed in her room. On her way she called Danny once but there was no answer. But a minute later came a WhatsApp message saying he was in a shoot and would call her at night. Reading the message she did feel bad that she hadn't responded positively when he had messaged her a few days back when she was in Meghna's flat. She didn't even know if Nitya was still living with Danny or not. It was not that if she wasn't, Rivanah would go back to live with him again. Somehow, living in the flat alone now, she was having contradictory feelings. A major part of her was happy to get a private space for herself where Danny and Nitya were no longer in her sight. That somehow plugged her insecurities to some extent. It made her happy. But she was also scared because she didn't know whether she should be really happy about it.

She yearned for Danny's lap, but she didn't want to call him. She wanted him to realize it and come to her. And the last few messages between them told her it wasn't going to happen anytime soon.

'They say my tea has magic in it.'

Rivanah was startled by the sweet voice she heard. She immediately sat up on the bed. By then the tube light had stopped flickering and was on. She saw a young girl standing by her bedroom door with a smile which was even sweeter than her voice. She was slightly frail but had a radiant face and looked like she was twenty or twenty-one years old.

'Who are you?' Rivanah asked.

'Tista Mitra. I shifted here this afternoon.'

'Oh, hi. I'm Rivanah Bannerjee.'

Tista came forward and shook Rivanah's hand.

'Nice to meet you, Rivanah di. I'm lucky to get a Bong roomie. Should I prepare my magic tea? I think you need it.'

There was a pleasant aura about Tista which Rivanah found herself envying instantly. An aura which existed only in those people who were yet to lose their innocence, who had not seen the ugly face of life like she had a year and half back.

'It's okay. I don't—' Rivanah started but was cut short.

'I will make it for myself anyway.'

'Okay.' Rivanah found herself smiling at someone after a long time.

Tista disappeared into the kitchen. Rivanah washed her face and went to the drawing room to find Tista sitting on the couch, stirring one of the two cups of tea with a spoon.

'Here,' she said, holding a cup up for Rivanah. The latter took it and sat down beside her. She was about to sip the tea when Tista stopped her, saying, 'The first sip should always be with eyes closed. Your system should feel that something amazing is going to invade it.' Tista herself took a sip closing her eyes. Rivanah did the same. The tea definitely had something different in it. It made her feel refreshed with the first sip itself.

'Isn't it good?'

Rivanah nodded with a smile.

'It is wonderful!' She was happy to have someone who made her smile for a change.

'Are you from Kolkata, Rivanah di?'

'Yes. And you?'

'Same. But originally I'm from Tezpur, Assam.'

'Working or studying? You look very young.'

'Thank you. I just turned twenty-two. I'm working in Stan Chart. What about you?'

'I'm in IT.'

The more Rivanah started knowing Tista, the more strongly she realized that Tista was what Rivanah had been a year back: naive, simple and ignorant. And because she was all those things she seemed happy all the time. Had she not come across someone like her, Rivanah would have concluded happy people didn't exist.

Tista worked as a relationship manager and had fixed working hours. She was there in the flat when Rivanah left and she was there before Rivanah came back. Though Rivanah hadn't opened up much to her, with each passing day, Tista did so without much fuss.

Neither of the girls entered the other's bedroom without knocking. This was something Tista did to begin with, which Rivanah followed because she liked it. No matter how close one gets to someone, they should always respect the other's privacy. One night, however, was an exception. Rivanah had left a particular book on the dining table but couldn't find it.

'Tista, did you see the book I put on the dining table?' Rivanah said, pushing the door of Tista's room open to see her lying on the bed in front of her laptop. Tista looked at Rivanah once and then at her laptop screen to say, 'My roommate is here. Give me a minute.' Tista climbed down the bed and came to Rivanah.

'I have the book with me.' She picked it up from the table beside her bed and gave it to Rivanah who took it without much curiosity about who she was speaking with. Half an hour later, when Rivanah was reading the book in her room, she heard a knock.

'Yes, Tista.'

Tista came in and sat beside her roomie on the bed.

'It was my boyfriend.'

'Huh?' Rivanah didn't know what she was talking about.

'When you came to my room I was Skyping with my boyfriend.'

Skype . . . boyfriend . . . it wasn't an unknown territory for Rivanah but it was definitely one she did not want to think about.

'It's okay,' she said, hoping Tista wouldn't prattle further on the topic.

'I love him a lot.'

'That's good,' Rivanah said and wondered why Tista wasn't shutting up. She was in no mood to discuss boyfriends.

'But I find him very cold towards me,' Tista said. A silence fell which told Tista that Rivanah was trying to understand what she had told her.

Novoneel Chakraborty

'Doesn't he love you?' Rivanah found herself asking.

'He does. I'm sure he does, but there's something that stops him from surrendering to me completely.'

'Where did you guys meet?' It was for the first time since they met that Rivanah had asked her new roomie a personal question.

'Actually, we are engaged. He is my fiancé. It was an arranged thing which our parents decided.'

'Nice.'

Some people go the simple way by letting the parents choose their life partner, Rivanah thought. And probably that's better than trying to go after the illusion of getting Mr Right and ending up in a shit pool like she was in.

'Can you please guide me, Rivanah di?' Tista said, breaking Rivanah's trance.

'Guide you?'

'This is my first relationship. And I really don't know what guys want or like when they are in a relationship.'

Tista's innocence made her wonder: how nice it would be if Rivanah too could marry the one with whom she was in a relationship for the first time! Suddenly that fairy tale called first love seemed so painfully desirable.

'Why don't you talk it out with him?'

'I tried to, but he says all's good and that he loves me a lot.'

'Hmm. Are you sure there's no other girl involved?' This came out straight from her experience. A year back she wouldn't have asked Tista such a question.

'I trust him.'

Rivanah looked at her for a moment. That was when she fully realized the difference between Tista and her: Rivanah could no longer say that for anyone even if she wanted to. A momentary sadness clouded her but she was careful not to let it show.

'How long have you guys been in a relationship?'

'It has been three months since our engagement.'

'When is the marriage?'

'Early next year.'

Rivanah thought for a while and said, 'I think you guys should know each other more. Maybe he is the kind who takes time to open up.'

'You know, I also thought of this. Thanks for confirming my idea. I am ready to give him all the time he needs,' Tista said with a smile. 'You read now; I'll leave.' She was about to move out when Rivanah stopped her, saying, 'You are a very good girl, Tista. I am sure the guy is lucky to have you in his life.'

'I hope he knows it too,' Tista said.

That's the problem with guys: they rarely realize how lucky they are when they get the girl who is perfect for them, Rivanah thought and smiled back.

With Tista gone, Rivanah put the book aside. The thought that her notice period had begun in office was a torment. And worse she had nobody to share her stress with. She picked up her phone and messaged Danny. He was supposed to call her but he hadn't.

Do we need to take appointments now to talk to each other? she messaged.

What she actually wanted to say was: *Asshole, call me. I want to talk.*

Danny's response came in the next instant: *Sorry, was busy the whole day.*

Rivanah's next message read: *What did you have for dinner?*

What she actually wanted to say was: *Is Nitya still there with you?*

Danny responded: *Ordered from Faaso's.*

Rivanah replied: *Hmm.*

What she wanted to say was *Why can't you just tell me if Nitya has left or not?*

Danny messaged: *What else?*

Rivanah's replied: *I shifted to a new place.*

What she actually wanted to say was: *Look, I don't need you all the time for everything.*

Danny's response read: *Good.*

Rivanah thought: *You won't even ask me where I'm staying? Great!*

136

But she messaged back: *What else?*

Danny's reply came in a second: *Nothing.*

What Rivanah thought while reading it: *Why can't you simply ask me to meet up? I will come, but just ask me first.*

Rivanah messaged: *Okay.*

So the cold war continues, Rivanah thought and stretched herself on the bed.

'Yippee!' Suddenly Tista barged into her room.

'Shit, Tista, you scared me!' Rivanah said, sitting up once again with her heart suddenly beating fast.

'I'm so sorry. Actually my fiancé is coming here tomorrow. He stays in Navi Mumbai. I'm so excited.'

'All right. That's nice. Now may I please sleep? I have office tomorrow.' Rivanah knew her rudeness was an outcome of the frustration that her current equation with Danny was brewing in her. Though Tista didn't show any sign of hurt, Rivanah herself felt bad. The next instant she went and apologized to Tista in her room. And asked what the plan was for tomorrow.

'I don't know. We don't like to go out much. Probably we will be in the flat itself. Let's see,' Tista said.

The next day Rivanah went to office and applied for some job openings on various job portals. Her notice period was on and she desperately hoped she could secure another job before it was over. In the evening she returned to her flat and saw that Tista wasn't there. On other days, she was the one who reached first and kept her magic tea ready for both of them. Rivanah didn't care to prepare any tea for herself and changed to lie down on her bed. She received a call from Tista.

'Look at my luck. My fiancé is coming today and of all days I am loaded with work today.'

'When will you be free?'

'Around nine. I think I will be at the flat by ten. My fiancé will be there in half an hour or so. Hope it is not a problem.'

'It is perfectly fine. I have reached the flat so he won't have to wait outside. Don't worry.'

Rivanah cut the line and checked the time on her phone itself. It was 7 p.m. She decided to cook for herself. Around 7.35 p.m. the doorbell rang. Rivanah went to open the door. Her blood froze when she saw the visitor. She realized he too had a similar expression on his face. He was talking on the phone.

'Yeah, I have reached. Yes, okay.' He handed the phone to Rivanah and mumbled, 'Tista wants to talk.'

She took her time to take the phone with her heavy hands and spoke into the phone, 'Hello.'

'Rivanah di, that's Ekansh, my fiancé. I shall be home soon. See you both.'

16

The moment Tista ended the call Rivanah dashed to the kitchen without saying a word, leaving the main door open. Standing in the middle of the kitchen doing nothing, she heard the main door lock. They were alone in the flat now. The last time they were alone in a flat she had lost her virginity to him. The scene flashed in front of her in disturbing detail. The last time she saw him was in Oberoi Mall where she had lost a life to him. And of all people Ekansh had to be Tista's fiancé? How can a cheat like him marry a naive soul like Tista? Trying not to think, she moved towards the oven.

'I'm sorry,' she heard Ekansh say. *Why was he even talking to her? Couldn't he just pretend they were strangers until Tista comes?*

She could sense he was standing by the kitchen door. His sorry still sounded the same. Fake. Why did she expect anything about him to have changed by now? With her back to him she didn't know if he was looking at her or not. For a moment she did try and look from the corner of her eyes. He was looking at her. Then she sensed he was moving towards her. Out of sheer nervousness, she tried to light the gas burner. She wanted to scream out to him to stop and not come close, but she didn't. She couldn't. She saw a reflection on the tiles in front of her. Ekansh was right behind her. The next moment she felt his breath on the back of her neck. All her muscles stiffened. She couldn't even press the lighter's button.

'I'm sorry,' he said almost into her ears. With all her energy she pressed the lighter button again and the burner lit up this time. She felt a hand on her waist. Rivanah immediately turned around to stop whatever she sensed could begin.

'Ekansh, we shouldn't . . .' She wanted to say more but he stopped her with a kiss. Right, wrong, should, shouldn't—the lines between them were blurring. She started to live in the moment and thus welcomed Ekansh's initiation by putting her arms around his neck. She wasn't waiting to kiss him all this while and yet she smooched him hard as if she was hungry for it. As if she was claiming him back in her life with it. As if through the hard smooch she was asking him: how dare you left me? As if she was trying to spin the wheel of time back and by the time the smooch would end they would realize they were still a couple, faithful to each other. She felt his hand on her butt as he lifted her up. She reciprocated by wrapping her legs around his waist. He carried her to her bedroom. It was dark and hence they could be what they were not in the light of the kitchen. In no time their skin was exposed to the other. Rivanah was surprised how deep the echo of the friction of their skin still reached her. And this surprise was the best aphrodisiac she had ever encountered. There was a hunger in Ekansh that matched hers in intensity. She would have stopped everything if she knew there was life waiting after this, but their mutual affinity convinced her otherwise. And sometime in the darkness when Ekansh was inside her she did hear him gasp, 'I love you.' The worst part was she was moaning out the same words. And with each thrust all the good times they shared in the past flashed in front of her. Every time she felt his mouth sucking her breasts Ekansh's face from college came to her. Every time his mouth caressed her lips she was convinced their break-up was only a bad dream.

It was almost an hour later that they moved away from each other, still lying in bed half naked.

In the silence of the room Rivanah could only hear their breathing. And the sound stifled her.

'Please leave the room,' she said, not sure whether she was angry with him or herself or with life or love. Ekansh stood up after some time, pulled on his underwear, got into his jeans and, adjusting his tee, was about to move out when the doorbell rang. Both Rivanah and Ekansh knew who it was.

Ekansh went to the drawing room and opened the front door. It was Tista who had excitement written all over her face.

'I'm so sorry to be late,' she said, spreading her arms and preparing herself for a hug.

'It's totally all right,' said Ekansh, hugging her and speaking into her ear.

She stepped into the flat holding his hand and closed the door behind.

'Your bus reached earlier than I thought it would.'

Ekansh gave her a tight smile and said, 'Yes.'

'What happened? You seem a little . . . off.' She looked into his eyes. He averted his eyes.

'Nothing. It is really nice to see you.'

'Same here. Did you have tea?'

'Not yet.'

'Wait, I'll make some.'

'You must be tired. Freshen up first.'

'It's okay,' Tista said with a smile that said she was already refreshed seeing him. She went to the kitchen and came out immediately.

'Where's Rivanah di?'

'Hmm?' For a moment Ekansh thought Tista had said, 'Why Rivanah?'

'My roomie. Didn't you meet her?'

Tista went to the kitchen. Ekansh was about to say something when Rivanah came out of her room in a different dress. She joined Tista in the kitchen.

'Hi.'

'Did you leave the burner on?'

'Oh shit! I went inside to change and forgot about it.'

'It is okay. I'm preparing my magic tea for us.'

'I'll make it.' Rivanah took over from Tista.

'Thanks,' Tista said and, turning towards Ekansh who had joined them, said. 'Even you haven't changed. I thought you reached here a while ago.'

'I was waiting for you to come back.' His voice betrayed guilt.

Rivanah called Tista to the kitchen when the tea was ready.

'We don't have a problem if you join us,' Tista said.

'Another time.' Rivanah made it sound as warm as possible. Tista was about to go into the drawing room with the two cups of tea when Rivanah asked her, 'By the way, how did you know about this flat?'

'As in?'

'I mean, who gave you a lead to this rented flat?'

'An agent called me saying someone told him I was looking for a flat.'

With bated breath Rivanah asked, 'Who was that someone?'

'I don't know. I didn't ask.' Tista shrugged and said, 'Why are you asking suddenly?'

Rivanah nodded, saying, 'Just like that.'

Once in her room Rivanah pushed the teacup aside. By then she had guessed it couldn't be a coincidence that Ekansh was Tista's fiancé. In fact nothing that had happened to her in the past year or so had been a coincidence. Tista was sent as a roomie to Rivanah so that she could meet Ekansh again. So that she slipped. She picked up her phone and messaged the stranger: *Why did you do this to me? WHY? Wasn't it enough that I resigned from my job? Ekansh and I fucked each other as if there was no before or beyond.*

She sent it to all the saved numbers in her phone but a response came from only one of them: *I only guided Tista to your place. The rest you did to yourself.*

Don't pretend you didn't know Ekansh wasn't her fiancé, an angry Rivanah was typing on her smartphone with hot tears in her eyes.

I told you to choose your god wisely, Mini. I only knew you were confident about your god. And I wanted to test your confidence.

Which god you are talking about?

Our god is what we think we are, and our demon is what we actually are. We are often blind to the difference till a situation brings it up. And I told you earlier, Mini, to choose your gods wisely. You chose loyalty as your god. Somewhere you thought you were loyal. Now it is time to face your demon. What you actually are.

I didn't want to do it. Trust me, I really didn't want to. I love Danny very much.

Now you are choosing convenience as your god, Mini.

How will I face Danny? How will I look at Tista? What will Ekansh think of me? And how the fuck will I look at myself in the mirror? Though the questions were for her, she typed them and sent them to the stranger as if it was her deep-seated conscience she was talking to.

Don't you think it is time to accept the obvious? You genuinely love Ekansh. You always did, you always will. Love is about attachment, Mini. You understand attachment? It is that chain which even if you break free from, or think you can, you will never be able to do anything about the marks the chain leaves on you. Those marks you take to your grave.

The message made Rivanah sob profusely. She didn't know what was more disturbing: that she still loved Ekansh, or that she would always love him, no matter what. What was more disgusting: that Danny may or may not have cheated on her, or the fact that she had already cheated on him? Which was filthier: the presumption on which she had initiated a cold war with Danny, or the lie she had used to convince herself that Ekansh was no longer important?

There was a knock on the door.

'Rivanah di, what should we prepare for dinner?' It was Tista.

Rivanah didn't move for a moment. Tista knocked on the door again. Rivanah rubbed her eyes and abruptly stood up. She took a few steps to open the door. And immediately hugged Tista tight. The latter didn't know why Rivanah did that. She still hugged her back as a reflex.

'I'm sorry, Tista. I'm very, very sorry.'

'Why are you crying, Rivanah di?'

'I'm a bad girl, that's why.'

Tista broke the hug and looked into her roomie's eyes which spoke of only thing: contrition.

17

'Any problem?' Ekansh came into the small passage between the drawing room and bedroom with a concerned face. He paused, seeing Tista and Rivanah in an embrace. Tista turned to look at Ekansh and said, 'Rivanah di is crying.' There was a momentary locking of gaze between Rivanah and Ekansh. Her eyes had a story. His had the moral of that story.

'I left the burner on,' Rivanah muttered. Tista looked at her in disbelief.

'Oh God!' Tista said with one hand on her forehead. 'You have been crying for that? Come on, Rivanah di.'

'There could have been an accident,' Rivanah said.

'Accidents are not in anyone's hand,' Ekansh replied, looking at Rivanah cautiously.

'But one should be alert especially if there already has been an accident in the past,' Rivanah said.

Tista glanced once at Ekansh and then at Rivanah, with no clue what they were talking about.

'I think I have a solution to this. How about I prepare a lovely dinner for us all?' Tista said, displaying her cute smile to the full.

'No, I will,' Rivanah said.

'You cook?' Ekansh blurted.

'Why do you sound surprised?' Tista asked. 'Rivanah di cooks better than I do.'

Rivanah didn't wait to listen to her praise. She simply walked towards the kitchen, saying, 'You two carry on. I'll tell you when dinner is ready.'

'Let me change and freshen up quickly. Then Ekansh too can change,' Tista said.

Rivanah went into the kitchen. Ekansh stood still for some time till Tista locked herself in the bathroom. Then he ambled to the kitchen.

'It is so nice to know that you can cook now,' Ekansh said.

Rivanah pretended she didn't hear him. Pretence was the only jacket she had to save herself from the winter of guilt. Ekansh stood there for some time and then said, 'Won't you even talk to me?'

'There's nothing to talk about, Ekansh. Not now. Not any more,' Rivanah said without looking at him. She was chopping an onion.

'I'm in need of someone who is ready to listen,' Ekansh said softly.

Rivanah gave him a sharp glance and said, 'Why? Are you now done with Tista because we just met and fucked and you enjoyed it so much that now you think you are in love with me again?'

The spite with which she spoke was enough to silence Ekansh. He turned and went back to the drawing room. Rivanah ate her meal separately even though Tista pestered her several times to join them.

Next day in office she received a call from Danny. She wanted to pick up but an ineffable fear stopped her from answering. She was wondering if she should call back when he called again. This time she took the call, pressing the phone against her right ear.

'I want to meet you,' Danny said. They were talking on the phone after quite some time. And with those words Rivanah understood the worst had already happened. The stranger must have told Danny about what exactly had happened between Ekansh and her in the flat. She shouldn't have blurted that out in a fit of emotion to the stranger. Screwing her up emotionally was the stranger's favourite pastime. This she was sure of by now.

'Are you listening?' Danny said.

'Yes. I have some work . . .' Rivanah's attempt to postpone the meeting sounded pretty unconvincing.

'It's important.'

Rivanah couldn't remember the last time Danny sounded so grim over the phone.

'Where?' she asked.

'Candies, Bandra. Around seven in the evening.'

'Okay.'

'All right, see you.'

He cut the line. *What do I tell him? That whatever the stranger had told him was rubbish? There couldn't possibly be any proof of it unless there were hidden cams in the flat. Were there?* Rivanah held her head which had started to throb slightly. One of her colleagues came and asked her if she had got through any company. She shook her head. And followed up with all the job portals and consultants through phone and mail but there wasn't any opening that suited her profile. Frustrated, she continued working with no interest in work whatsoever.

In the evening Rivanah reached Candies on time and found Danny already waiting for her. They were seeing each other for the first time after Rivanah had walked out of the flat. He looked preoccupied. She didn't know if he had already noticed that she wasn't looking directly at him.

'How are you?' she said, sitting down opposite him.

Danny only took out a large envelope and put it on the table without saying a word. Rivanah frowned. *Were there photographs inside? The damned stranger* had actually sent Danny photographs of Ekansh and her together? With trembling hands she took the envelope, opened it and took out its contents. There were papers. Legal papers, she noticed. In fact, stamp papers on which was an agreement between a production house and Danny. She looked directly at Danny for the first time in the evening. He was already beaming.

'I have got a movie deal finally!'

'Oh wow!' Rivanah couldn't control her instinctive reaction and she half rose from her seat to hug Danny and congratulate him.

'Though it is not the lead, the production house is good and I'm sure the role will lead to better deals.'

'I'm sure too. I'm so happy,' Rivanah exclaimed. For a moment she actually thought all her problems were solved and that life was smiling at her. Then Danny grasped her hand tightly and said, 'I'm sorry for the last few weeks.'

She swallowed a lump.

'I know I ignored you,' Danny said and continued, 'but I wanted to surprise you with this. The production house got in touch with me a day after you left. I was waiting for the contract to happen. They gave it to me last night.'

Rivanah managed a tight smile. She wanted to know if Nitya was still there with him but somewhere her guilt told her she had lost the right to ask Danny about Nitya.

'Nitya has left too,' Danny said, as if reading Rivanah's mind. 'In fact, I asked her to. I know you were never comfortable with her around. But I hope you understand, being her best friend, I too was duty-bound.'

'I understand,' Rivanah said, her throat feeling bone dry. She turned around and asked a waiter to bring some water for her.

'So, when are you coming back?' Danny asked with that typical charming smile of his which time and again made her feel funny between her legs.

'I have just paid all eleven months' rent. I don't think the landlord will refund it,' Rivanah said and noticed disappointment eclipse Danny's face. He slowly pulled out his hand from hers. Did she say so because she actually wanted to stay away from Danny or did she say it because now she knew she could be close to Ekansh? It was one of those grey questions which one never asks oneself, and if one does, then one evades the answer at any cost.

'Or else I would have,' she said but this was more of an attempt to convince herself that she wasn't choosing Ekansh over Danny. Had she not given the rent she would have definitely shifted, she thought once again.

'Okay. You can always come over, right?'

That I'll anyway have to whenever Ekansh comes to meet Tista, Rivanah thought, and said, 'Yes.'

'Or maybe I could come over,' Danny said with an amused face. She knew what he was hinting at.

'I have a roomie at my place. So, it'll be better if I come over,' she said and shuddered at the thought of what would happen to her if and when Ekansh and Danny were in her sight together.

'That's cool with me as long as you are near me,' he said and leaned forward to whisper, 'I love you, Rivanah.'

Rivanah kept looking at him.

'Why are you crying?' Danny asked. She didn't know when her eyes had flooded.

'Any problem?'

Rivanah nodded and carefully pressed a paper napkin against her eyes so that her eye make-up didn't smudge.

'Did that bugger disturb you again?'

Rivanah paused and looked at him inquiringly.

'The stalker,' Danny clarified.

Should she tell him the stranger had compelled her to resign from the job, had manipulated the situation in a way that she ended up fucking Ekansh?

Rivanah nodded. The stranger may have made her resign but the latter happened because of her own indiscretion. It had to happen, it didn't matter that she had met Ekansh a day before or was meeting him in the future.

'Let's go.'

'But we didn't order anything,' Rivanah said.

'Doesn't matter. I have tickets for the night show of the new Hobbit sequel. Let's get going.'

As Rivanah stood up, Danny held her hand. That one gesture made her feel relieved as well as protected. As if her demons wouldn't be able to get to her in Danny's presence. Danny was almost pulling her along when she called out to him. He turned.

'I love you, too,' she said. Danny came close and, in full view of everyone, caught her lower lip between his lips and sucked it for a few seconds. He looked at her. Rivanah wondered if he had tasted her or tasted Ekansh through her. He smiled and the question lost its relevance in Rivanah's mind for the time being.

They reached the multiplex in the nick of time. In the dark theatre Rivanah kept glancing at Danny time and again. She was happy the cold war between them was over. She was saddened by its timing. If Danny had met her a day or two earlier, she wouldn't have done what she did with Ekansh. It was irreversible. But so was her love for Danny. The stranger had told her she genuinely loved Ekansh and hence she couldn't get over him. Did that mean she had never loved Danny truly? That was absurd because she was ready to marry him, to fight with her family to be his. Would anyone do that if he or she wasn't truly in love?

'I need to go to the washroom,' Danny said and went outside. Rivanah toyed with her phone and then, unable to resist her urge, messaged the stranger. After all she was the one supposedly suffering from the Cinderella complex. And the stranger was one helluva mystery prince.

What exactly is cheating in a relationship? Rivanah messaged.

The response came a little earlier than she anticipated:

Your answer is waiting in the third toilet inside the men's washroom beside the multiplex entrance.

It could only mean the stranger was in the washroom right at that moment. There was no way he could guess her question. He must be writing the answer there right now for her to find later. Rivanah sprang to her feet and scampered out of the theatre. She walked briskly to the first washroom by the entrance. The door had a man's silhouette pinned on it. All shows were on and nobody was either going in or coming out. She held the doorknob, looked around, took a deep breath and pushed the door open. There was nobody in sight. She entered the washroom. And then she saw someone peeing with his back to her. The guy turned and shrieked.

'What the fuck are you doing here?' Danny said.

Shit! Rivanah thought. In the utter excitement of getting to the stranger she forgot Danny had excused himself to the washroom. She had to tell him something, anything but the truth.

'What are you doing here?' she said, feigning surprise.

'It's the men's washroom.' Danny, done answering nature's call, turned to her.

'Oh! I thought this is for girls,' Rivanah said. She was about to turn around when the door to the third toilet opened. Rivanah paused, holding her breath. Danny followed her eyes and looked at the door too. And then at the guy who came out of the door. He didn't know him. Rivanah did. It was Ekansh. She instantly turned around. Her heart was racing like never before and she could feel her body shudder.

'I'll see you outside, Danny.' She rushed out of the men's washroom. She hoped Ekansh had not seen her. But what was he doing there? Or was it another of the stranger's sadistic manipulations?

Rivanah came out of the men's washroom and went straight to the girls' washroom. It was empty except for her. She wasn't able to think properly. The fact that Danny and Ekansh were right there in front of her together had made her go blank. She heard the washroom door being pushed open. It was a female cleaner. She came right up to her and handed her something, saying, *'Kya yeh aapka hai? Darwaze ke pass pada tha.'*

Rivanah looked at the white piece of cloth which the female cleaner was holding. She took it from her and opened it out to read the only word written on it in black thread: *LOL*.

18

The first thing Rivanah did after coming back to the theatre with Danny by her side was message Tista to ascertain if she was with Ekansh or not. She was. The film was ruined for Rivanah. She knew Ekansh was there with Tista in another hall watching another film. It stressed her out to think: what if Danny and Ekansh came face-to-face once again while exiting?

'Did you see anyone else when you went inside the washroom?' Rivanah asked Danny in a whisper. He gave her a curious look and said, 'Anyone else?'

'With long hair?'

Rivanah had Argho Chowdhury in mind. Danny frowned for a moment and said, 'Nope. I only saw the guy who came out of the toilet when you were there.'

Rivanah immediately averted her eyes from Danny, knowing he was talking about Ekansh.

'Why do you ask?'

'Just like that. A friend messaged me saying he was here with his girlfriend.'

'Oh, okay.' Danny said and went back to watching the movie. Rivanah didn't like the fact that she had to lie to him. But she knew this was probably the beginning of a series of lies. Why couldn't she simply turn and tell Danny she had cheated on him but it wasn't planned, it wasn't something she thought she would do? It simply happened. He loved her, she loved him. He would understand her. The momentary slip on her part wouldn't affect their relationship. In fact the confession would only cement the break in the relationship which at present only she could see.

'Danny . . .' she blurted, turning towards him.

'Hmm?' He turned towards her. Eye to eye. And the guilt pulled her will to tell the truth somewhere deep within her.

'I'll be back,' she said instead.

'Don't get into the men's washroom again,' Danny said with an amused face. Rivanah gave him a tight smile and stood up. Soon she was out of the theatre. She felt weak within. She sat down on one of the stairs outside, burying her face in her lap. Her phone vibrated with a message. She lifted her face and read it.

People think cheating is an action like sleeping with someone, kissing someone or whatever. Wrong. Very wrong. Cheating is when you feel the pressure of being faithful to someone because of someone else. When you suddenly realize there's an option. That realization is cheating.

A couple of teardrops fell on her mobile screen. Another message popped up. It read:

You are a cheat, Mini.

Rivanah buried her face in her lap again and sobbed. A couple of passers-by did notice her but nobody approached her. Her phone beeped with a WhatsApp message.

Where are you?

It was Danny. She replied: *Coming.* Rivanah wiped her tears, regained her composure and went back inside the theatre.

From the time Danny dropped her at her place that night she wanted to leave Tista and shift to another flat where there was no Ekansh and no Danny. But she had already paid her eleven months' rent which also put pressure on her savings. While signing those cheques Rivanah had had a job. Now she had resigned; she was yet to appear in any interview; and she had only three weeks before she was totally jobless. She felt like a fort that was being attacked from all sides and, though it was standing its ground, Rivanah knew it would be taken over soon. And she had no idea what she would do then. She made it a point to tell Tista to inform her in advance whenever Ekansh was coming over so that she could give them the privacy every couple needed. She now knew from Tista that Ekansh had shifted from Bangalore to Pune and now to Navi Mumbai. He generally came over on weekends. But he didn't stay over. Was it because he too was as sorry as her for whatever happened? Did he tell Tista about it? On the one hand she was avoiding Ekansh because he knew too much about her, while on the other she started ignoring Danny because he knew too less. Though Danny too didn't have time owing to the new film he had signed, she started saying no to him whenever he asked to meet up. Holed up inside her flat alone, Rivanah first tried listening to music at full volume and cooking. It didn't help. She needed something more visually engaging. She watched all the latest American sitcoms till the wee hours of the morning every day, plugging her ears and fixing her eyes on the laptop screen. The content seldom registered with her, but she still used to follow the serials because it somehow kept her mind distracted from the emotional hurricane that ravaged her heart. In office, she lost her interest in work. Every time she sat down to work she knew time was running out. Soon she would have no office to work in. She kept applying to other places but in vain. The only time she forced herself to smile was during the two-minute phone calls to her mother after reaching office, after lunch and post dinner. She developed dark circles in no time and also lost five kilos in twelve days. Her appetite for life was waning. One evening she ended up writing a suicide letter as well, but she tore it up knowing she wouldn't be able to do it. She sat down to watch yet another television series when she realized it could no longer keep her hooked. Time and again her thoughts went back to the fact that she was a cheat. That something which she hated in people had become her definition now. It disgusted her. Tista only acted as a reminder whenever she came to her and tried to talk about what Ekansh and she did. Rivanah tried her best not to sound rude and pretended to listen to whatever she said, but in reality she began to shut herself out. One night while she was idling in her room, Tista came in and said, 'I need to talk to you, Rivanah di.'

There was a grimness in her voice which Rivanah rarely associated with Tista. She only gave her a silent glance. That was enough for Tista to come and sit on the bed.

'Ekansh is still in love with his ex.'

Rivanah could almost feel her heartbeats stop suddenly. Then she relaxed. She was *one* of his exes.

'How do you know?' she asked.

'I don't know. I feel it at times. Like last weekend he and I were in Marine Drive, and we were getting into the mood but suddenly he went off. I asked him but he said the place reminded him of someone else.'

Chances were it was Rivanah he was missing, she thought.

'Who is it? Did you ask him? Did he mention any name?' Rivanah asked.

'No. I thought he may get upset. His past isn't something I should be concerned about, I think. I'm sure if I had a past, I too would have reacted in the same manner.' Tista thought for a moment and then said, 'Can I ask you something, Rivanah di?'

'Hmm.'

'If you had a past would you share it with your boyfriend or keep it within you?'

Each word of that question injured her. She was too stifled to even frame her thoughts.

'Oh wow!' Tista, said catching hold of the electricity bill behind which Rivanah had been sketching.

'I never knew you could sketch too.' Rivanah didn't even realize when she had grabbed a pen and had started to sketch on the bill.

'I didn't know either,' Rivanah said and looked at the sketch. It was a pair of eyes. *Not bad for a first-time sketcher*, she thought. The good thing was that the sketch took

Tista's mind completely away from the question Rivanah dreaded not only to answer but even to consider.

That night, instead of watching yet another TV series, Rivanah sat down to sketch. She used to sketch as a teenager too but she didn't know when she grew out of it. And now sketching a pair of feet, with focus, she felt energized after a long time. Revelling in the rediscovery of her lost hobby she forgot that the day after was going to be her last day in the office. She was reminded of it when she was given a farewell lunch by her teammates the next day. When she came back to her apartment, the security guard handed her an envelope. By the time she reached the elevator she had already taken out its contents: a cheque for fifty thousand and one hundred rupees. The exact amount she was left with in her savings bank account. There was no signature in the cheque nor was there any name written on it.

'Hello, Mini.' Someone spoke the moment she stepped inside the elevator and closed its doors. She turned around in a flash. She looked at the floor of the elevator where there was a mobile phone on speaker mode. She picked it up and said, 'What is it now?'

'You sound as if you are angry with me.' The voice didn't sound like it had the last time.

'You haven't given me any reason to be happy with you,' Rivanah said as the elevator stopped on her floor.

She stepped out.

'The choices were yours, Mini.'

'Yeah, sure. And you had nothing to do with my choices. Anyway, just tell me, what is it?' Rivanah said, pacing up and down her corridor. She knew something was up. The cheque and its amount couldn't be a coincidence.

'I want you to sign the cheque.'

It was then Rivanah realized the cheque was from her own chequebook. Her account number was printed on the left side.

'How did you get my chequebook?'

'I have my ways, Mini. Just sign on it.'

'Who is it for? And why would I sign it? It is my money. The last of my savings.'

'You will sign it because I want you to.'

'You want me to go back to Kolkata, don't you? Why don't you say it?'

'Write on the name section: Mr Dilip Rawat.'

'Who is—?' she was about to ask when the line was cut. A baffled Rivanah kept staring at the cheque.

19

After entering her flat, Rivanah was about to chuck the envelope with the cheque in it when she found a SIM card inside. She immediately put it in the phone she got in the elevator. The SIM memory contained a few messages which she read one by one. The first message had an address of a certain Dilip Rawat. It was an apartment in Borivali West. *But why the cheque?* Rivanah wondered, slumping into the sofa. If the stranger wanted money from her then why would he wait till now? Was this Dilip Rawat a way to divert the money to Argho? If the stranger was Argho then he obviously wouldn't give his true name to her. If this was true then whoever this Dilip Rawat was, he was linked to the stranger or Argho as well. And if it was all because of squeezing money then the stranger could have threatened to share the video he had made long back; there was no reason for him to wait this long when he knew she had given more than half of her savings in rent. Rivanah held her head, trying to think as she scrolled down to another message stored in the SIM. It had Tuesday written on it and a specific time. So, Rivanah thought, the stranger wanted her to deliver the cheque to the address on Tuesday—which was the next day—at 1 p.m. Did she have the option to say no to the stranger? Not as long as he had her video, she told herself. After the attack on her by the stranger in her flat and the subsequent filming of it, Rivanah wasn't confident about going to the address alone but she was curious. She called Danny immediately and asked if he was free in the afternoon.

'So Ms Busy Bee finally found time to meet me,' Danny said. His sarcasm didn't hurt Rivanah for it was justified. It had been more than a fortnight since they met, when they had watched the movie together. She always gave him some excuse or the other and postponed their meeting. Danny's presence brought her guilt to prominence as much his absence blurred it.

'I'm sorry, Danny. Been a little hectic, that's all.'

'When did I complain? I'm free tomorrow afternoon. Where should we meet?'

'Pick me up from my place around twelve. We need to go somewhere.'

'Where?'

'To a friend's place,' Rivanah said cautiously.

Next day afternoon they headed to IC Colony in Borivali West. Danny parked the car inside the complex. It was the second building from the main gate they had to go to. Rivanah and Danny together climbed up the stairs.

'So you won't tell me why we are here?'

'Told you. I have to give this to a friend,' Rivanah said, flashing an envelope she took out from her bag.

'All right.'

They were on the second floor. The second flat from the stairs. Rivanah looked around for the doorbell. Danny spotted it first and pressed it. They heard the bell ring distinctly. Half a minute later the door was opened by an elderly gentleman. He looked at Danny and Rivanah in a way as if he was sure they had lost their way.

'What is it?' He said. His voice quavered.

'I was asked to deliver a cheque to Mr Dilip—'

'Oh! Please come in. I'm so sorry to have kept you waiting.'

Danny and Rivanah shared a glance and stepped inside the flat.

'Give me a moment, please,' the man said, closing the front door and then he disappeared inside.

Everything in the flat seemed old and untouched. There were lots of photographs on the wall. A particular one caught Rivanah's eye. It was a picture of a boy along with a lady and the man who opened the door for them. Danny was by then ensconced on the sofa. He pulled her by the hand and made her sit too. The next second the man who opened the door came out with an elderly lady who smiled at them. The two sitting on the sofa smiled back. Rivanah guessed she was the lady in the photograph. The elderly lady came and sat by the sofa in front of Rivanah.

'How is my son?' she asked, still smiling, looking at Rivanah and Danny alternately.

Which son? Rivanah for a moment was clueless. She noticed the elderly lady was still looking at her expectantly. She looked at the man. He looked a little tense.

'I don't know . . .' Danny started but was cut short by Rivanah.

'I'm your son's friend. He is doing fine,' she said and saw how the man too smiled now.

'I told you he is fine. Just that these days work is so much that he doesn't get time to come and meet us. But he will be here soon,' the man told the lady.

'Only I know how difficult it is for a mother to keep waiting for her child.' The woman sighed, looking at the floor. 'Anyway,' she continued, 'at least this time Arun sent his friends, otherwise it is always some errand boy delivering the cheques.'

'Did you say Arun?' Rivanah asked.

'Yes. Didn't Arun send you?' the woman asked.

'He did. But we call him by his nickname so I got confused.' Rivanah gave an unsure smile and thought hard. No, she didn't know any Arun. Something about the elderly woman told her it would hurt her if Rivanah was honest with her about having no clue about her son.

'I had given the nickname. Though he doesn't like it much.' The woman had a nostalgic smile on her face. Then she looked at Rivanah and said, 'What will you have? Tea or—?'

'Nothing, Aunty. We are—'

'They will have tea.' This time the man spoke a little assertively. The woman looked at him and said aloud, 'Let me prepare it.' She got up and went to the kitchen.

The man came and sat down adjacent to Rivanah. He looked at her and said, 'Thanks.'

'What happened?' she asked.

'I don't know whom to thank. I was a junior-level government employee. Now all I have is a meagre pension, no medical cover and literally no savings. Whatever I had invested in my son's education, thinking . . .' He was too choked to speak. 'Every three–four months someone or the other keeps coming with the cheque. And thus my wife and I continue to survive.'

'Are you . . .?'

'I'm Dilip Rawat. And I know you aren't my son's friend nor has he asked you to bring in this cheque.'

Rivanah's lips slowly parted. *Does he know the stranger then?*

'But Aunty said it is Arun who sends the cheques.'

The man looked at the floor for a moment and said, 'My son Arun died few years back.' He kept staring at the floor as if he had just got the news.

Rivanah and Danny shared an awkward glance.

'We are sorry to know that,' Danny said and made a mental note to ask Rivanah about the matter. *If Arun was dead then why did she not know about it, since she said it was a friend's place they were visiting?*

The man suddenly looked up at them with a smile and said, 'It is okay.' The smile curtained a pain. 'The problem is, my wife doesn't know about it,' he said.

'She doesn't know her son Arun is no more?'

'She once did. But the shock was too much and she developed Alzheimer's in no time.'

'The disease where you lose your memory?'

The man nodded.

'I have packed roti and aloo-matar for your tiffin,' the woman cried out from the kitchen. 'Take a bath now. I'll look after the kids.'

The man looked at Rivanah and said, 'She doesn't even remember I have retired from work.'

171

'Why don't you tell her?' She asked.

'I need to go after lunch today,' the man said aloud to his wife who was still in the kitchen. Rivanah got her answer.

'Where do you go if not office?' Danny asked.

'I travel from here to Churchgate on the local train and then roam about here and there. And then come back home on time in the evening.'

'But how long do you think this will go on?' Danny asked.

'I don't know. I'm okay even if I can keep her away from reality for one more day. You see I told her something years back. I'll do my best to live up to it.'

'What did you tell her?' Rivanah said curiously.

'That I love her.' The man sounded slightly choked again but he controlled himself well. The reason the stranger sent Rivanah here slowly dawned on her.

'Don't you wonder, Uncle, who these people are who bring you the cheques?'

'I only know that there are still good people in this world.'

Rivanah understood that the stranger asked people to visit with the cheques, pretending to be Arun's friends. Just like he had sent her.

Mrs Rawat came out with tea and some snacks on a tray. Rivanah and Danny had it with Mrs Rawat talking for most of the time. Before Rivanah left she gave the cheque to the man, Dilip Rawat. She had only one thing on her mind: with the delivery of the cheque she had officially become broke. What was she going to do?

Danny asked her if he should drop her to the office. In order to not arouse his suspicious she agreed.

'So, who is this friend of yours whom you don't know and yet you went to give money to?' Danny asked while driving her to her office.

She knew this question would come. She was ready with an answer that wouldn't raise further questions.

'Arun's friend is a friend. I thought it was his place.'

'And the money?'

'The friend will return it.'

'Okay.'

This was one thing Rivanah always liked about Danny. No complicated questions. He was always satisfied with what she told him. Would he be all right if she told him the guy in the multiplex toilet the other day was Ekansh, her ex? That he was now her new roomie's boyfriend? And that he fucked her the day they met in the flat with her giving in to him so easily, something she would have never thought possible?

Danny dropped her right in front of the office building and went off to his film's acting workshop. She was wondering if she should go back to her flat when she got a call from a private number. She picked it up on the fourth ring.

'Let's have coffee together, Mini,' the stranger said.

For a moment Rivanah didn't know what to say. Then she said, 'Yeah, right.'

'I'm serious. Krishna Towers terrace in half an hour?'

Was the stranger seriously going to have coffee with her in Krishna Towers? Did he live there? Rivanah thought as she felt excitement run through her veins. She found herself saying, 'Yeah, okay.'

Rivanah took an autorickshaw and rushed to Krishna Towers. Fortunately for her there wasn't much traffic and she reached her destination a few minutes before time. She knew the terrace keys were kept with the security guard. She asked for it, citing the excuse that she needed to check her dish antenna.

'The terrace is open, madam. A few minutes ago a television mechanic took the keys to check the dish antenna.'

Was it really a mechanic or . . . the stranger? Before the guard could say anything more Rivanah dashed inside the apartment building, took the elevator to the fifteenth floor—the topmost floor—after which she climbed a set of stairs to come face-to-face with the terrace door. It was indeed open. She checked her watch. One minute left for it to be half an hour since the stranger had cut the phone call. She took a deep breath. One more step and she would be able to see the stranger. Rivanah exhaled and crossed the terrace door to step onto the terrace. She looked around. There was nobody. She heard a phone ring. She followed the sound and reached a corner away from the door where a mobile phone was lying on a table. A private number was flashing on it. Rivanah picked it up.

'Hello, Mini.'

'Where are you?'

'Look to your right.'

Rivanah obliged but still couldn't see anybody. The stranger asked her to look again at the table on which the phone had been left. Rivanah noticed there was a pair of binoculars on the table. She picked them up and, as directed by the stranger on the phone, looked to her right again. This time she could see a figure on the terrace of one of the high-rises adjacent to Krishna Towers. Rivanah adjusted the zoom to the max but realized it still gave her only a vague outline of the person. She couldn't be sure if it was a man or a woman. If she ran out, she wondered, and got to the opposite terrace, by then the stranger would be gone. She could make out the person was waving at her. *Very smart!* she told herself as a smile touched her lips.

'There's more,' said the stranger. Rivanah found there was a cup of coffee right under the table, covered, so that it didn't lose its steam. She picked it up, all the while pressing the binoculars to her eyes. The person lifted one of his hands. She did the same, lifting the coffee cup up.

'So won't you meet me ever?' Rivanah said on phone.

'Only when the time is right.'

'And when shall that be?'

'You'll know.'

'Hmm. Thank you, by the way. Thanks for leading me to this amazing couple. Though I felt sad for them, I felt good about myself after a long time.'

'I had to do it.'

'Why "had to"?'

'How else would you have known that nobody is always good or always bad? For example, the girl who cheated on Danny is also the girl who is now the reason why the elderly couple shall survive for the next two–three months.'

A sadness eclipsed Rivanah's excited self. She removed the binoculars from her eyes, lost in thought.

'Have your coffee, Mini,' the stranger said.

Rivanah took a sip and said, 'Why did I slip in that moment in the kitchen with Ekansh? I was so sure I loved Danny till that slip.'

'We all have this special talent for hiding a truth by adding layers of lies on to it.'

'What's the truth?'

'That you genuinely love Ekansh. You can't escape it.'

There was a silence which Rivanah broke by saying, 'Does that mean the lie is I don't love Danny?'

'The lie is: you love Danny . . . only.'

Rivanah sat down on the table, holding her head. She wasn't able to think clearly.

'What should I do now?' she said in a choked voice.

'Ekansh already knows the truth. That you love him. It is time for Danny to know that as well. That you love him too.'

'But Danny knows I love him.'

'You have to tell Danny that you still love Ekansh, even if it means that you want to live with Danny.'

'That's absurd! I will never say that. Danny will leave me for sure. I don't know if you know this or not, but I'm not in touch with Ekansh after the kitchen incident.'

'When we hide something from our partner a part of us is never with them. And in your case a very important part won't be with Danny. Understand this, Mini: when you are attached to one and attracted to another, then one's truth becomes the other's lie as long as you keep the truth away from each other.'

'What if Danny leaves me? I simply can't take a break-up now. I'll die.' Rivanah's eyes had tears in them.

'From when did love start to concern itself with who is leaving whom? Love is whether someone truly belongs to someone or not, be it for a moment or for a lifetime.'

There was a prolonged silence. In that silence Rivanah understood she was staring at an abyss which was her life. Everything she thought was dear to her was finally gone. The last bit left was Danny.

'I will not only tell Danny the truth but also go back to Kolkata. I am anyway jobless and after Danny hears what I did I am pretty sure he will leave me. Mumbai won't have anything for me. Nor will my life.' She was sobbing by the end.

'Before you start to pack your bag, do check your email, Mini.'

The stranger cut the line. Rivanah immediately checked her email on the phone. What she read made her smile through her tears. She would have given the stranger a tight hug if he was near her.

20

The email was from the HR team of Zeus Technology Pvt. Ltd, asking if she would be available for an interview the next day. Reading the email Rivanah couldn't decide whether it was real or just one of stranger's jokes. She looked through the binoculars and was about to say something on the phone but the line was dead by then. There was nobody on the distant tower as well. To be sure Rivanah immediately called the HR's number that was provided in the email itself. They confirmed a time for an interview the next afternoon.

Rivanah thought of sharing the news first with her parents but stopped herself. It was only an interview. She must get an offer letter first, otherwise there would be a barrage of questions from her parents, the most important of which would be: first of all, why did you leave your job, Mini? She didn't want to share the news with Danny either till she had an offer letter with her.

Instead Rivanah shared the news with Tista on the phone right away. She had to tell someone about the interview in order to calm her thrilled self. She knew it was stupid because an interview did not necessarily mean a new job, but for her even this was welcome news.

'That's wonderful, Rivanah di! All the best,' Tista said, equally excited. Rivanah adored how genuine Tista always was. Whatever she said or did was straight from the heart; no filters, no pretension. Like she had once been. It also made her sad because the kitchen incident wasn't only about cheating on Danny. It was also about cheating on Tista and the bond they had formed as roomies. What would happen if she ever came to know about it? *She too will have filters from then on*, Rivanah answered herself in her mind.

'Thanks,' Rivanah said.

'But I will need a treat.'

'It is only an interview. I haven't got the job yet.'

'You will. I'm sure,' Tista said. Rivanah only hoped she was right.

The next day Rivanah reached Zeus Technology's office on time. Zeus was in Mindspace, Malad West, and it was not as big as her previous office. She remembered the place well since she had been here following Argho once. Would she stumble upon him again? This was the first time she was going inside the building. She found out that Neptune Solutions was two floors below Zeus. Once on the desired floor Rivanah was asked to wait for fifteen minutes after which a junior HR came, the one whom she had already spoken to, and set her up with a technical person who interviewed her for close to an hour. Once it was done, the same HR junior told her that she would be interviewed by a senior at 2.30 p.m. Though Rivanah wasn't hungry, she couldn't resist the idlis a vendor was selling just outside the building. She ordered a plate and was promptly served steaming idlis with a dash of coconut chutney. She finished her food and was wiping her hands using a tissue paper, when her phone rang. It was Danny.

'Hi, I have something to tell you,' he said.

'What happened?'

'I will tell you when we meet. Let's have dinner tonight.'

He had sounded the same when he had surprised her with the film contract. Was it a surprise again or . . . ?

'Okay,' she said.

'I will message the place. Be free around eight.'

'Sure.'

Danny didn't ask her more. *I have something to tell you . . .* Rivanah feared the worst. It could either be about Nitya or maybe the stranger had told Danny the truth before she could. Her phone rang again but this time with a landline number. It was from Zeus. Her interview was about to start in a few minutes. Rivanah rushed inside.

She was asked to wait in one of the glass-walled cabins where she would be interviewed. She looked around. Everyone seemed to know exactly what they were supposed to do without a hint of bother on their faces. Rivanah prayed she would get through the interview. Suddenly she sniffed something. Just Different, Hugo Boss. Her heart started racing and precisely then she heard someone say, 'Hi.'

Rivanah turned her head to see a clean-shaven man with long hair which was tied in a pony, sporting carbon-framed glasses. Before she could notice any other feature her jaw had already dropped. It was . . .

'I'm Argho Chowdhury. Senior HR at Zeus.' He extended his hand.

What the hell is he doing here? Isn't he with Neptune Solutions? Rivanah thought without knowing she was looking stupid. Argho shrugged, waiting for her to stretch her hand and shake his hand. Rivanah slowly lifted her hand. They shook hands. He sat down on a chair right beside her.

Argho took a moment to check all her certificates, payslips and other documents to see if everything was in place. While he was doing so Rivanah kept wondering if the man sitting only inches from her could be the stranger.

But why was he acting like he had never seen her before? Was it because he didn't know she had tracked him to Neptune Solutions before and followed him some time back? Or was he actually a damn good actor?

'Weren't you in Neptune Solutions before?' Rivanah blurted out. Argho stopped leafing through her documents and looked at her. It was obvious what he was thinking: *how do you know?*

'I'm sorry. What I meant was I gave an interview for Neptune Solutions too and someone there resembled you,' Rivanah quickly improvised. It wasn't convincing enough.

'I'm sure I'm meeting you for the first time though I did work for Neptune Solutions till a month back,' Argho said and went back to her documents.

'I'm sure you are,' Rivanah quipped, thinking how well he was faking it. And it would be better if she played along too just to be absolutely sure whether Argho was the stranger or not. She was itching to ask him about Hiya as she clearly remembered he had written 'RIP Hiya di' on her profile. But she knew this wasn't the time. One little slip and she could very well spoil her chance of solving the mystery behind Hiya Chowdhury for ever. Perhaps, she wondered, Argho was her only chance.

Argho Chowdhury asked her a few basic HR questions at the end of which he offered her the position of senior programming analyst with a salary hike of 45 per cent over her previous job. He said she would get an email with the offer letter the same evening and she would have to revert by the next evening. The rest of the formalities would follow once she accepted the offer.

'Have a good day, Ms Bannerjee. Hope to see you here,' he said and turned his chair around to face the table. Rivanah took her documents and left. Before she left the HR space she turned back to look at Argho. She quickly averted her eyes because he too was looking at her.

Finally, relief! She wouldn't have to go back to Kolkata just yet. There were two other things she had on her mind. Argho came to this company a month back. And now she would too join. Was it a ploy by the stranger? Or should she say *Argho*?

Once outside Zeus, she entered the elevator with two men and a lady. The men stepped out on the floor below while the woman stepped out a few floors before ground level. Rivanah was now alone inside the elevator. She was trying to check her email when the 3G connection failed. Then the network too was wiped out. She waited for the elevator to reach its destination. It didn't. It suddenly stopped and the lights went out simultaneously. Rivanah immediately remembered how the stranger had done the same thing in her Goregaon apartment once. She started banging the closed elevator door with force while crying out for help. She could hear people outside as well. Someone asked her to back off if she was near the door since they were opening it from outside. Rivanah shouted back to them that she was away from the door. The elevator door was manually opened. What she saw was a tall guy in a blue formal shirt neatly tucked into his black trousers. He had a strong jawline, and a sharp nose and chin. His hair was thick. His eyes were a bit greenish. The man was looking at her expectantly. It was then she realized the elevator had stopped at quite some height from the floor. She would have to jump down.

'You can jump. It's safe,' the man said. He had sexy voice. And an infectious confidence. Even if she knew she would be hurt, she would have still jumped because of this man's confidence. Rivanah bent down slightly, hurled herself into air and landed right into the man's arms. The way his hands squeezed her muscles while holding her evoked a feeling of desire. The man quickly placed her on the floor.

'Thank you,' Rivanah said.

'You are welcome,' the man said and walked off briskly. Rivanah couldn't help staring after him in a schoolgirlish way. Once he was gone she took the stairs this time.

Later in the evening Rivanah reached Hawaiian Shack at Bandra. Danny had told her he would join her there. She didn't know what it was he wanted to talk about, but her mind was busy with what the stranger had told her: *When we hide something from our partner a part of us is never with them*. And, to be honest, Rivanah wanted every part of hers to be Danny's. She felt an arm around her. Before she could turn, Danny planted a kiss on her cheek and took the seat in front of her.

'Here,' Danny said and put an envelope on the table. It was way smaller than the one which had the movie contract.

'What's this?' Rivanah said, a little wary of opening the envelope.

'See for yourself.' He was still not giving her any clue.

Rivanah slowly drew the envelope towards her and opened it, still looking at Danny sceptically. She looked down and broke into a huge smile. It was a cheque. Danny had officially secured his first film. Rivanah leaped up and hugged Danny tight.

'Congrats, baby.' She kissed his cheek.

'Thank you so much. I was so waiting to see this reaction of yours,' Danny said, kissing her on her lips.

They settled down in the chairs after a prolonged hug.

'I am feeling so alive right now,' Rivanah said.

'So am I.'

Rivanah picked up the seven-lakh cheque in her hand and looked at it closely.

'Let's celebrate by being together. It's been a long time!' Rivanah said.

'I have something on my mind.'

'Like what?'

'You'll see. Get a leave tomorrow. The acting workshop is closed tomorrow but day after I will be busy with it again. So let's make use of tomorrow.'

As Danny talked on about leave Rivanah quickly checked her email on her phone. There was a mail from Argho Chowdhury: the offer letter. Before reading it herself, she showed the attachment to Danny.

'New job?'

'A 45 per cent hike! Do I need to give any other reason?'

'Double whammy!'

'I was so waiting for this offer to happen.'

'Now we better celebrate tomorrow our way.'

'Sure,' she said and sent a confirmation email immediately. She looked up at Danny and saw he was going through the menu. Should she tell him the truth? Rivanah wondered. They were so happy right now; what if the truth disturbed this state? No, this was not the time to spill out the truth. They drank, had dinner and danced a bit too, all the while Rivanah convincing herself that the time for not right for the truth. When they came out of Hawaiian Shack, they walked for a few seconds to reach a little lane where Danny had parked the car. They got in.

'Where's my phone?' Danny said. Rivanah had no idea.

'Shit! I guess I left it inside. Give me a second.' Danny went to get his phone. Sitting alone in the car in the quiet street Rivanah called her mother and told her that she had finally hopped to a better job with a higher pay package. She also told her about Danny's success at securing a film. Her father wasn't in; her mother said she would convey it to him first thing when he came home. As she was talking she heard someone bang the back of the car.

'Mumma, I'll call you later.' Rivanah cut the line and turned. There was nobody. It was the first time she realized how quiet the lane was. She leaned out of the window to get a better view. At that instant someone banged the front windshield of the car. Rivanah turned in a flash. Her heartbeat suddenly quickened. There was a vehicle in front whose headlights were switched on and the light fell right on her and thus she could only see a silhouette in front of the car. Was it Argho? She swallowed a lump, shielding her eyes from the headlight. Was the stranger going to tell Danny the truth? She felt fear tightening up her muscles. And what followed made her go numb. The figure broke Danny's car's windshield with one single blow. With squinted eyes she tried to see who it was, pieces of glasses all around her. She shut her eyes again. She knew how to unbuckle the seat belt but she wasn't able to move. The other car's headlights went off. There was no figure visible now as Rivanah opened her eyes completely. Rivanah was about to open her seat belt when she noticed a white cloth on her lap.

Certain lanes are so attractively safe that we don't realize when it leads us to a busy highway. And it is only then that we have to decide whether to cross the highway or not. It is a decision that is seemingly momentary but is actually life-altering. When will you cross the highway, Mini? When will you tell Danny the truth? I won't repeat my question.

'What the fuck happened?' It was Danny. Before saying anything Rivanah grabbed the white cloth with the message, hiding it from him.

21

Rivanah lied to Danny that it was an urchin who had hurled a brick at the car probably assuming there was nobody inside the car. When she screamed the urchin had run away. Though Danny didn't quite get why someone would do such a thing, he didn't probe any further. He drove immediately to a service station where they asked him to leave the car overnight so that the windshield could be fixed.

'Are you sure we shouldn't report it to the police?'

Rivanah gave Danny a sharp glance, trying to understand if he had unmasked the fact that she had lied to him about the urchin. But she wasn't sure. Perhaps the fact that she had not let go of Danny's arm from the time he came back to the car after fetching his phone told him that she was indeed scared.

'That won't be necessary.'

'Hmm, okay. Can't you stay at my place tonight? We are leaving for Khandala first thing in the morning anyway. We are going to a resort.'

This made sense to her. Staying with Danny would be the perfect cushion for her fear. The aggressive move from the stranger had seriously rattled Rivanah. Was it necessary? She would have anyway told Danny the truth. Would she have?

'That sounds good to me. Though we will have to go to my place in the morning to collect my clothes,' Rivanah said.

'That's fine,' Danny said and called out to a cab. Rivanah called Tista but she didn't pick up. She left her a message that she would come to the flat in the morning.

An hour later she stepped into the same flat from which she had moved out many days ago. It brought back memories for Rivanah. Nitya wasn't there any more. As she looked around she heard Danny say, 'Nitya is in Paris with her designer boss.'

She liked the fact that Danny had clarified the matter without her asking the question.

'Hmm,' Rivanah said, moving into the bedroom.

'Can't we pretend the Nitya episode never really happened?' Danny said, coming into the bedroom after her.

Can't I pretend Ekansh didn't happen to me? Rivanah wondered and said aloud, 'I have something to tell you Danny.' She was facing him. He came a tad closer and said, 'What is it?'

Should she say it now? Rivanah kept looking at Danny hoping that he would simply read her mind and understand her heart without her having to use words to express it aloud. Danny shrugged.

'I love you' was all she could come up with.

'I love you too,' Danny said and hugged her tight. And in the embrace Rivanah understood that a simple truth carries the potential of destroying a relationship in a far more irreversible way than a complex lie. Sleep was a far cry for Rivanah and she spent the whole night staring at Danny who slept soundly.

In the wee hours of the morning Danny and Rivanah went to her flat. She didn't see Tista there, which seemed odd to her. She wasn't the kind of girl who would not come home at night. Maybe she had gone to Ekansh's place. At least she should have intimated her about it, Rivanah thought, and called her once again while packing her stuff. The call went unanswered while she realized she was yet to get a response to her last night's message to Tista. Rivanah messaged her again, asking her to call or message back as soon as she read her messages. Done with packing Rivanah left with Danny for the service centre from where they got their repaired car and then drove to Khandala. On the way she kept wondering that on the one hand she loved Danny—she knew it—and on the other she was questioning the authenticity of that love by not sharing an important happening of her life with him. Her only excuse for it: how will he react? What if the truth triggers an emotional landslide? The fear of consequences—is it too part of loving someone with all one's heart? Or is love about being fearless even it means choosing your own doom? They reached the resort close to afternoon. They freshened up, had a sumptuous brunch and then they were back in the room.

'I have something to tell you.' Rivanah summoned all her energy.

'What is it, honey?' Danny said and came to rest his head on her lap, looking at her directly. All of Rivanah's resolve went away.

'I love you,' she said, disappointing herself.

'I love you too,' Danny said and kissed the tip of her nose, raising his head a bit and closing his eyes. As Rivanah caressed his hair he said, 'Life seems so peaceful right now.'

Should she tell him the truth and rob him of the peace? Rivanah wondered and looked down to realize Danny was asleep. She rested her head back while continuing to run her fingers through his hair. Rivanah slept like a log. When she woke up she found herself lying on the bed alone. She sat up. The sound of water was audible to her. She looked around but Danny was not in the room. The digital clock in the room displayed the time—11.15 p.m. *Shit! I slept for ten hours.* Rivanah got down from the bed and, putting on her slippers, went towards the balcony from where the sound of water was coming.

Rivanah stepped outside the room. It was relatively quiet. The distant view was of covered mountains and a silence which had a sheath of moonlight over it. There was nobody in sight except for Danny taking a bath under the open sky shower at the edge of the balcony. A naughty smile escaped Rivanah as she saw the water from the shower cascade down Danny's naked back. The next moment Danny turned around.

'I knew you would come,' Danny said with a tempting smile that Rivanah read as an invitation to join in. The sight of Danny showering alone stark naked aroused her after a long time. She moved towards the shower and stopped. Their eyes remain locked while their faces had a tinge of naughty amusement. The steam around the shower area told her the water was warm. The way it was trickling down Danny's naked body made her already slightly wet between her legs. A small light was on right above the shower which covered that particular area with a bluish light. Rivanah could see the details of Danny's nudity. It had been some months since she had seen him this naked. With eyes fixed on Danny, Rivanah first stepped out of her slippers. The ground below was cold. It added to the sensual feeling which from a brisk wind had turned into a storm now. She raised her arms next and took off the black top she was wearing, to expose her black bra to Danny. The top was dropped on the ground. She tilted her head, unbuttoned her white capris and pulled them down seductively. She stood there, looking teasingly at Danny. With a sexy pout Rivanah took her hands to her back and unhooked her bra. Before she could drop the bra on the floor Danny came out of the shower. He came to her, smooched her hard and then, kneeling down, tore her panty off. Then he rose and picked her up. He took her under the shower. Rivanah by then had surrendered totally to him.

The extreme passion with which Danny made love to her under the shower was something she had never experienced before. It was as if he was sucking the soul out of her and making it a part of his. Since it was an open shower, there was no wall for support on either side. They were each other's support and it made the sexual act all the more intimate. With Danny's hands supporting her butt she wrapped her legs around his waist and her arms around his neck. As he finally penetrated her, she reached the zenith of pleasure. In the distance she could see the mountains, moon, some clouds, trees . . .

darkness beyond them. And each of them seemed to be talking to her.

You love Danny . . . you should tell him the truth . . . you love Danny . . . you shouldn't tell him the truth . . . tell him the truth . . . shouldn't tell him the truth . . . the truth . . . truth . . .

'Will you marry me, Rivanah?' Danny said, pushing himself deep in her and digging his teeth into her shoulder. It was the most intense marriage proposal she knew of. She yelled out in pleasure and pain and said, 'Yes, Danny . . . I will, Danny. I will.'

A prolonged moan and a grunt escaped both Rivanah and Danny respectively as they climaxed together. By then she had scratched his back to her heart's content. He had even bitten her lips, sucking the blood from it. Finally, as he came inside her, he let her feet down on the floor. They stood in a quiet embrace with the warm water gushing over their intertwined bodies. Sometime later Danny broke the embrace, saying, 'I'll wait for you inside.' And he ambled away to the room. Rivanah switched off the light, shivering a bit in the coldness of the night. She was about to move out when a light fell on her. For a moment she thought the shower light had been switched on but in a flash she realized it was not the case. The light that was on her came from a distance beyond the fence of the resort where there were some dense bushes. Rivanah was quick to cover her privates with her hands.

'Is that you?' Rivanah blurted, knowing well who it could be. Had he been watching her copulate with Danny all this while?

The flashlight went off for a second and was on again. *So he is talking in binary. Off means a yes, on means a no*, Rivanah thought. Would the stranger come out in the open now? It wasn't the first time the stranger was seeing her naked. She couldn't see much in the light. Or in its absence, when it was abruptly switched off. *Was it really Argho standing a few metres from her?* This was her best chance to unmask the stranger. And the only way to do so was . . . seduction. The fact that she was naked was also her power. She stood her ground firmly with no more communication from the stranger except for the flashlight which was on at that point of time. Rivanah closed her eyes and with a shiver slowly raised her hands, exposing her privates and saying aloud, 'I'm . . . all yours, stranger. Come, take me.'

Rivanah was sure the seduction would work. She waited with bated breath. *Was Argho approaching her?* She couldn't tell. Her eyes were closed, senses alert and muscles tense. She was praying for the stranger to come to her. She was craving to open her eyes and see the stranger's face and confirm her suspicion that it was Argho. Seconds became a minute but nobody approached her. The flashlight was still on. Driven by impatience

Rivanah opened her eyes and was dumbfounded with horror. A noose was hanging from the shower right in front of her. The stranger had tiptoed right up to her and she hadn't even realized it. The flashlight went off. In the darkness Rivanah's voice returned to her and she yelled out to Danny. He rushed out of the room.

'What happened?'

Rivanah swallowed a lump. By then she had pulled down the noose and thrown it away into the bushes in the dark.

'Bring me a towel please.' She knew she was unconvincing but it was still better than telling him what had just happened. It wouldn't help her cause if Danny knew the stranger was still stalking her.

They drove back to Mumbai the next day. When Danny dropped her by her apartment building he asked, 'Can't you shift back?'

Rivanah only wished she could say yes, but the distance that the stranger had talked about, she didn't want to kill it just as yet. That distance was giving her the space to place her guilt. Staying together would only nurture it.

'Give me some time,' she said. Danny nodded, saying, 'I'll wait.' He drove away.

Rivanah unlocked the door and stepped inside the flat, only to hear someone weeping inside Tista's bedroom. It sounded odd. More so because it wasn't Tista but a man.

'Who is it?' she said, not closing the front door. The next moment Ekansh came out to the drawing room, rubbing his eyes. This was the first time she had seen him crying this way.

22

'What happened? Where is Tista?' Rivanah said, trying to look beyond him and hoping Tista was there as well. She didn't want to be alone in the flat with Ekansh. The latter simply sat down on the couch, hiding his face with his hands, and said, 'She is not here.'

'Why are you crying? What's wrong?' Rivanah was herself surprised with the genuine concern she showed for him. Some people will burn your world into ashes and yet the smoke from the singe would still be in love with them, Rivanah thought.

Ekansh sat still for some time and then said, 'I can't live without her.'

Rivanah sensed the obvious. Tista must have left him just like he had left her a year and a half ago. A sense of satisfaction invaded her. Tista didn't look the type who would ditch a guy, but if she really had ditched Ekansh, it must be his fault and not hers.

'She is your fiancée. Who is asking you to live without her?' The last part was deliberate. If Tista had left him then it would hurt him. Rivanah wanted that. At that moment she only wanted to hurt Ekansh. She closed the front door, feeling confident of the fact that there wouldn't be any more slips on her part. Ekansh's weakness was her source of confidence.

'She is not well,' Ekansh said, still not looking at her.

'As in? What happened?' Rivanah preferred to stand against the wall facing Ekansh.

'She has acute pancreatitis and some problem in her small intestine as well.'

'What are you saying? She never told me.' Rivanah took her phone and immediately called Tista. A phone lying beside Ekansh began to ring.

'What the . . .'

'She left her phone with me.'

'What? Why would she do that?'

Ekansh looked up at her and said, 'She used to save voice notes on her phone.'

'What voice notes?'

'About her thoughts on us.'

'Us? She knew about you and me?' Rivanah's heart was in her mouth.

'Us as in Tista and me.'

'Oh, okay.'

There was silence. *Did you ever cry for us, Ekansh, like this after we broke up?* Rivanah wanted to ask. *I did*, she wanted to confess. Instead she spoke aloud, 'Has she gone for a check-up? When is she returning?'

'She is in Kolkata. She may not return even if she becomes all right. I came here to give the remaining rent cheques from her side and the flat keys. Here . . .'

He gave the cheques and the keys to Rivanah. She took them quietly. She didn't know how to react. She was feeling bad for Tista, but for Ekansh . . .?

'You know,' Ekansh said, 'before you came here I was on the phone with her. She asked me what I would do if she died.'

'But why would she die?'

'She may have to undergo a surgery soon and the doctor said there's a 70 per cent chance she may not . . .' Ekansh didn't say the rest.

'I want to talk to her now.'

'She is sleeping. I will arrange for you to talk to her when she wakes up,' Ekansh said and hid his face with his hands yet again. Rivanah was about to ask Ekansh if he needed some water when he spoke up, 'Life has been tough since the time I wronged you.'

Rivanah shot him a sharp glance. For the first time she heard him clearly accepting that it was he who had ditched her. No excuses, no reasons. A simple confession.

Till then all Rivanah had wanted to do was laugh at his situation. But the moment he confessed she felt like forgiving him. Not for what he did to her but for what he did to himself, perhaps, after what he did to her.

'I realized I made a mistake when Vishakha left me for someone else like I left you for her.' Ekansh was talking with his face in his hands while Rivanah was listening with her eyes closed and resting her head on the wall.

'I still don't know why I chose her over you. I was so happy with you. Maybe I was happy with you but I wasn't happy with *us*. Those are two different things. People jump into a relationship when they experience the former.'

Rivanah was itching to ask if he really thought they had jumped into a relationship and maintained it for over four years without it being genuine. But she kept those words to herself as she heard him say, 'After Vishakha left me I was pretty sure I would never fall in love again, for I understood that, if I could never appreciate the kind of love you had for me, I probably didn't deserve to be in love.'

Rivanah could feel tears oozing out from her eyes but she knew it was futile to wipe them away. Even if she wiped those tears out she could never suppress the feeling which was triggering them.

'Then Tista happened to me. She was the younger sister of one of my colleagues. I went to his place in Kolkata last Durga Puja. We met there. Since our parents knew each other, the proposal came from her parents and my parents accepted. I honestly didn't care any more whom I got married to. We were soon engaged. I discovered the best part about Tista was that she never demanded anything. She loved me. That's all. I wish I could love her or anybody else like that. So absolutely.'

I too loved you absolutely, Ekansh. And you are the reason why I won't ever be able to love someone else absolutely, Rivanah thought.

Ekansh stood up and said, 'I'll ask Tista to call you from her father's phone when I talk to her next. I'm taking her things with me.'

'Won't she come back?' Rivanah asked.

'I hope she does. But she would need rest so I asked her to resign for the time being.'

Ekansh went to Tista's room once again and reappeared with a suitcase.

'Thanks for listening,' he said and left.

Rivanah sat still, fervently wishing that Tista came out of the surgery alive and healthy. For the first time after her break-up with Ekansh she prayed for him too. Sometime later she freshened up and left for her new office.

In the office she had to meet the junior HR to talk about her leaves and submit hardcopies of some documents. The truth was Rivanah actually wanted to see Argho. Her plan was simple. She wouldn't let him know she suspected him. The irony was she had to meet him as a stranger to know if he was the real stranger or not. She asked the junior about Argho.

'You can tell me whatever it is. He hasn't come to office yet,' the junior said.

'It is okay. I will wait for him.'

'He isn't well. He was absent yesterday too.'

Rivanah's jaws dropped. He was absent. Did he follow her to Khandala?

'In case he comes in I'll tell him,' the junior said.

'No, no, it's all right. Don't tell him anything,' Rivanah immediately blurted. The junior gave her an as-you-wish shrug.

It was during her post-lunch casual walk around the office building, while talking on the phone with Danny, that Rivanah noticed Argho entering the office premises.

'I will call you in a bit, Danny,' she said and cut the line. Rivanah rushed inside the building and saw Argho taking the stairs. *Is he going to climb the eleven floors?* She reluctantly took the stairs as well.

As she reached the first floor she saw Argho move out of an exit door. She reached the door before it closed and found herself staring at a corridor which led to the emergency backstairs. *Should she or shouldn't she?* Rivanah decided in a flash and took the emergency backstairs like Argho who by now had already climbed a floor. Since these were the backstairs there wasn't anybody there. She could hear Argho's footsteps climbing up. She took care he didn't get an idea someone was following him. On the fifth floor Rivanah slowed down, typed a 'Hi' on the message section of her phone and sent it to all the numbers she had of the stranger. She raced up and could see Argho standing on the seventh floor checking his phone. She checked her phone. One of the numbers had a delivered tick next to it. *Damn!* She sighed. How she wished she could call the number. It would have been all clear if he was the stranger or not then and there.

Rivanah soon felt the fatigue and thus was taking her time to climb up. Finally she reached the office floor. She saw Argho had entered the door from where a corridor would lead them to the front stairs. Rivanah was exhausted. She took a deep breath and, summoning all her residual energy, climbed the last set of stairs to reach the door. She turned the doorknob but it didn't open. She turned it a few times and then her eyes fell on the red indicator on the right which would turn green only when a magnetic ID was tapped on it. And Rivanah didn't yet have her ID. Her breath was getting back to normal as she stood there thinking what to do. She turned back and got the scare of her life. A man was standing right behind her. Perhaps a finger away. As she pressed herself against the door, she realized it was the same man who had rescued her from the stuck elevator a few days back.

'I hope I didn't give you a fright,' the man said. There was an air of decency about him. And it was irresistible. He was tall, wheatish-complexioned and handsome, but Rivanah wouldn't have described him with these words to anyone. If she had to describe him it would be simpler than that. She would use the word 'sexy'. Period.

'I don't have the—' she started but the man took out his card and tapped it on the red light. It turned green. He pushed open the door.

'Thanks,' Rivanah said and thought: she had met this man twice now. And both times he had rescued her. *Who the fuck is he?*

'I'm Rivanah Bannerjee, Zeus Tech. I'm new here so I don't have a card yet,' she said, hoping he would introduce himself as well.

'Nice to meet you, Rivanah Bannerjee,' he said and walked away, pushing the door further. His secretiveness made it even more tempting to pursue him. She ran after him, took the corridor and reached the front stairs. He was nowhere. Rivanah went inside her office wondering why he hadn't introduced himself when something struck her. She had told the man she was new here. It reminded her of the offer letter. She opened her Gmail on her phone, opened her offer letter. It was from Argho Chowdhury. She scrolled down to the bottom of the email and checked Argho's signature. It had his name, his designation and . . . his phone number. She copied it, saved it on her phone and dialled. Her screen flashed the name Stranger 10. It was the tenth number she had saved of the stranger. Rivanah cut the line, feeling a chill down her spine. She was finally sure Argho was the stranger.

23

Rivanah didn't get a chance to get back to Argho throughout the day. She wanted to follow him in the evening as well to know where he lived. She wanted to know everything about the stranger as he did about her, before she revealed to him that she now knew who he was.

At seven in the evening she went towards the HR cubicles and noticed Argho was wrapping up for the day. She went out and waited by the elevator so that she didn't arouse suspicion. Even if he took the stairs, she would take the elevator and wait for him outside the office premises. This time Argho took the elevator. She stood right behind him. The scent of Just Different, Hugo Boss, coming from him and the thrill of knowing the stranger made her smile to herself. Ground floor. Argho stepped out. So did Rivanah.

She would have followed him and crossed the road, just like he did, had Ekansh, who was standing by a bike by the office building, not called out to her.

'Ekansh? What are you doing here? How did you know I work here?'

'Chuck that. I need to talk.'

Rivanah's focus was still on Argho, who had by then taken an AC bus and was out of sight. She averted her eyes to Ekansh.

'Talk about what? How is Tista?'

'Can we please sit somewhere?'

Rivanah looked at his troubled face. *I will never be able to say no to his face*, she thought, *all because, once upon a time, I loved this guy with all my heart.*

'Okay.'

Half an hour later, Rivanah found herself sitting with Ekansh inside a CCD close to her place.

'Tista didn't call me. I was waiting,' she said.

'Wait,' Ekansh said and dialled a number. They exchanged a look as the phone kept ringing.

'Hello, Aunty. Is Tista awake?' Ekansh waited and then said on the phone, 'Hi, all good? I'm good. Okay, talk to Rivanah.'

'Hi, Tista,' Rivanah said, taking the phone from Ekansh.

'Hi, Rivanah di.' Tista sounded pretty weak.

'You never told me!' Rivanah said.

'I'm sorry, Rivanah di. It all happened so fast.'

'It's okay. You just take care. We'll meet soon.'

'Will we?' There was a deep doubt in her voice.

'Shut up. We certainly will.'

'I hope so too. Can you go a little away from Ekansh?'

'Yeah, sure. Excuse me,' Rivanah said to Ekansh and went towards the washroom.

'Tell me, what is it?'

'How is Ekansh handling it? Like, he doesn't tell me anything and tries to make me laugh all the time but I know he is deeply affected.'

Rivanah took a moment to respond.

'He indeed is,' she said, feeling uncomfortable saying it. She didn't know the exact reason for it even though she knew what she told Tista was true. Ekansh clearly was affected.

'I knew it,' Tista said and added, 'Can you just tell him I love him more than anything else in the world? I won't be able to say it because, if I do, I shall break down on the phone and I really don't want to do that.'

For a second Rivanah felt choked. She looked at herself in the washroom mirror and realized her eyes were swimming with hot tears.

'Rivanah di?'

'Yes, yes, I will certainly tell him that. And don't you worry. No true love ever goes unfulfilled,' Rivanah said, fighting hard to believe it herself.

Rivanah came out of the washroom and gave Ekansh the phone.

'What happened? Why did you have to go to the washroom with the phone?'

'She loves you, Ekansh. She said she loves you more than anything else in the world,' Rivanah said. There was silence. Rivanah didn't look at Ekansh. How time changes the dynamics of a relationship, Rivanah thought. A year and a half back she was with Ekansh in Marine Drive and they were telling each other how much they loved the other. Now she was sitting right opposite him and informing him how much another girl loved him. And in between she supposedly went through the I-hate-you phase as well. A break-up doesn't necessarily end the love two people have for each other. In fact some love stories never end. They only end something within the people involved. Rivanah knew she was still in love with Ekansh and it didn't matter how much she denied it, because otherwise she wouldn't be sitting with him in the cafe. She looked up and saw Ekansh was looking out of the glass door with tears rolling down his cheeks. *Had he ever cried for her after their break-up?* she thought again and was about to pass on a tissue paper to him when she stopped mid-air. Something was written on the tissue. She read it: *Truth?*

Rivanah instantly turned to look around. Argho had not taken the AC bus. He must have followed her here.

'Did you see a guy with long hair in the cafe?'

'Huh?' Ekansh turned to look at her. He had no clue what she was talking about. 'No.'

'Did you leave the table at all?'

'I went to smoke outside when you were in the washroom.'

'You smoke now?'

Ekansh nodded. 'But what happened?'

Rivanah shook her head keeping the tissue with her while giving another one to Ekansh. He wiped his tears off and said, 'I know why I'm going through all this.'

'Why?'

'People who ditch true love once don't deserve to get true love again.'

Rivanah could sense a confession in Ekansh's words but didn't know what to say. The confession gave her as much pleasure as it pulled her emotionally towards Ekansh.

'I need you, Rivanah,' Ekansh said out loud. She wasn't ready for this. Even though she had suspected he may say it, she hadn't expected him to do so right then. What did he mean anyway by 'I need you'?

'Don't worry; I won't force this friendship on you. It will only happen if you want it too. None of my friends

213

know about Tista's condition except you. I don't feel like sharing it with them. I am too tired to unwrap myself in front of them. With you it is easier, you know me well already. I want you as my friend, Rivanah. Someone on whose shoulder I can cry. Someone with whom I can share my wounds. Someone with whom I can be emotionally naked.'

And what if our emotionally naked selves ask us questions we can't handle? The kind of questions which slowly deconstruct us and in the quest of finding answers to them we get constructed into someone we never thought we could be. The only question, at that instant, however, was this: was she ready for such a deconstruction?

Rivanah let go of a deep breath. She was about to speak up when she felt someone's presence by their table.

'Hey!'

Both Rivanah and Ekansh looked up. It was Danny. Rivanah's throat instantly went bone dry. *Had Argho told Danny the truth?*

24

'D anny?' Rivanah exclaimed and immediately knew she shouldn't have made her surprise so overt.

'As if you didn't know I was coming here. *You* texted me!' he said. He side-hugged her, planted a kiss on her forehead and sat down between her and Ekansh.

You texted me . . . Rivanah knew who this 'you' was. Argho was back to his sadistic best.

The next moment was the most awkward of Rivanah's life. She had her ex and her present boyfriend staring at each other for possible introductions.

'Danny, this is Ekansh. Ekansh, this is Danny,' she said. The men shook hands wishing the introduction was longer than that for them to know who exactly they were.

'Wait a minute,' Danny said and seemed thoughtful. 'Aren't you the guy from the washroom?'

'Which washroom?' Rivanah quipped.

'The multiplex washroom.' This time it was Ekansh.

'Yes!' Danny was happy that he was right.

'Ekansh is a good friend from college,' Rivanah told Danny and to Ekansh she finally turned and said, 'Danny is my boyfriend.' From the corner of her eye Rivanah saw Ekansh withdraw into himself on his seat. She had told him she was single. The silence that followed had a probing energy to it which made Rivanah uneasy like never before.

'So, why did you want to meet so urgently?' Danny asked Rivanah.

'Though of watching a movie,' Rivanah blurted.

'Christ! I thought it was something more serious. Anyway, am free. So we can go.'

'Yeah. Let's go,' Rivanah said and stood up.

'It was nice meeting you, Ekansh.' Danny said and, putting his arm around Rivanah's waist, was ready to leave.

'See you,' she told Ekansh. He only nodded with a tight smile. And watched her walk away with Danny.

In the next minute Rivanah was in the car with Danny. He was driving towards the nearest multiplex.

'Tell me something,' Danny said. 'Wasn't your ex's name Ekansh too?'

'Yes,' Rivanah said and hoped he would ask all the important questions she was running away from and all she would have to do was say 'yes' or 'no' and that would be the end of the story.

'Is this the same Ekansh?'

'Yes.'

'Were you looking for him in the gents' washroom that day?'

'No!' She glanced at him once.

'And today too you met him coincidentally?'

Rivanah didn't like his interrogating tone but she couldn't do much realizing that, somewhere, she deserved that tone.

'Pretty much,' she said. Danny didn't ask anything further. Rivanah zoned out during the whole movie, conscious at times of Danny laughing out. She did text Argho on all his numbers saying that she wanted to talk. She didn't care if it was Argho or not. She wanted a sounding board. But there was no response. After the movie Danny dropped her at her flat.

She skipped dinner and was busy sketching when she got a call from a private number. She put on her earphones and took the call.

'Hi.'

'Hello, Mini.'

For once she was tempted to say, 'Argho, please cut the crap and tell me it's you, because I now know it is you.' But she didn't say anything lest it disturbed her connection with him which, at that point of time, she was more in need of.

'I know you want me to tell Danny the truth and even I want to. But before I do that, I have a question for you.' Rivanah was furiously sketching as she talked over the phone.

'What's the question?'

'Why can't I love both of them?'

'You can but you will have to live with one of them,' promptly came the response.

'Who made that diktat?'

'People who tried to do what you now desire and failed miserably.'

'Is revelling in the attention you get from more than one person a sin? When Ekansh and Danny both had their eyes on me I felt powerful in a way I have never felt before.'

'Attention is an aphrodisiac, Mini. The more you get it, the more important you'll feel. The more important you'll feel, the less you'll know yourself.'

'But will I be very wrong if I claim such attention from both?'

'All of us define right and wrong in relation to the other. If this is right then that is wrong. That way nothing is wrong, nothing is right.'

'Then why do you want me to tell Danny the truth if nothing is wrong or right?'

'Some people can only be your horizon, Mini. You may crave them, you may burn, you may die but you will never get to them. But also understand this: when someone is your ever-eluding horizon, the sun of your emotions shall always rise and set in their lap. If that can't give you peace, nothing in love will.' The stranger spoke slowly, giving Rivanah the time for the words to register along with its subtext.

'You mean Ekansh is my horizon?'

'I mean either Ekansh or Danny will eventually be your horizon. You'll have to learn to live with it.'

'But before I know who that horizon is, why can't I have the attention of both guys? How do I know Danny has told me everything?'

Rivanah by then had finished sketching. It was a pair of eyes that she had sketched. She went towards the open window in the room and inhaled some fresh air. The phone call was still on.

'You can either give yourself excuses, Mini, or you can tell the truth,' the stranger said.

'I don't want to tell Danny the truth. Not right now.'

'Your yes or no will have consequences, Mini.'

'Why do I have to listen to you all the time? I have asked you a million times who Hiya Chowdhury is but you never tell me. I told you to meet me but you won't. But I have to do whatever you want me to. Sorry, but that's not possible,' Rivanah blurted impulsively. Why couldn't the stranger tell her that what she had in mind was perfectly all right? She heard the line go dead. For once she didn't care if the stranger was angry. She, after all, had the right to live her life the way she wanted. The rest of the night she continued to sketch without feeling sleepy.

Next day in office she kept wondering what was wrong in revelling in the attention she got from two people. It wasn't that she was interested in Ekansh sexually. The kitchen incident was a slip. Period. It wouldn't happen again, Rivanah told herself with confidence. Ekansh needed her as a friend. Danny needed her as a girlfriend. Why couldn't she fulfil both the roles without merging them? And then it struck her: Danny was perhaps doing exactly the same with Nitya when she had come to stay at their place. It had made Rivanah leave the flat. There was a greater truth that she had to accept before she told Danny about the little truth that happened in the kitchen with Ekansh. The greater truth was: she needed both the men in her life. Roles didn't matter, their presence did.

In the evening she received an email on her personal account. It was an invite for the convocation cum alumni meet of her college that was supposed to happen the following weekend. *Could it be another of the stranger's games?* She called Ekansh.

'Hey, did you get an invite for the convocation and alumni meet from our college?' she asked.

'Yes, I did. Few weeks back. It is next week.'

Rivanah was relieved to know it was a genuine invite.

'Oh, I got it today only. Are you going?'

'I'd anyway have to. I had applied for leave before. Tista is getting operated the next day.'

'Oh.' Rivanah took a moment to think and then said, 'When is your ticket? And which flight?'

'It is on the Friday night. Indigo flight.'

'Message me the details. I shall book tickets on the same flight if available.'

'Give me a moment.' Ekansh said. As Rivanah waited she thought her motivation to go to Kolkata wasn't the convocation or the alumni meet. She wanted to meet Tista once for sure before the operation but she also wanted to see if someone from Hiya's home was present at the convocation or not.

25

Danny dropped Rivanah at the airport the following Friday evening. He didn't ask if Ekansh was also attending the convocation; she didn't tell him either. She kissed Danny goodbye and entered the airport. She met Ekansh at the gate. Soon they collected their boarding passes, passed the security and boarded the flight.

'I want to thank you, Rivanah, for being there,' Ekansh said once they had taken their seats. He tried to grasp her hand. But she was alert. Anything that could lead to a probable slip turned her off. She withdrew her hand and said, 'I think we are meant to be in each other's lives always. If not as lovers, then at least as friends.'

The last part was deliberate. She wanted to underline the fact for Ekansh.

'Let's not go to the convocation together,' Rivanah said, looking out of the window.

'As in?'

'As in,' she looked at him, 'let's not enter together. Let's not behave like friends in front of everyone.'

Ekansh thought for a moment and then nodded, saying, 'All right.' He understood it would call for unnecessary questions that even he didn't want to answer.

Once in Kolkata they took separate cabs for their respective homes. She called her mother and told her she would be at home in some time. While she was talking she had received a message on phone. She read it after she was done talking to her mother.

Time's up, Mini. Now be ready.

Her throat dried completely as she read this. The last time the stranger had messaged 'Time's up', he had exposed Ekansh's infidelity. What now? Did she piss him off a little too much by not obliging him earlier? Was the stranger going to finally going to unveil Hiya's link with her?

It was a new number from which the message had been sent. She checked the number on the Truecaller app but it didn't show any record except that it was a Kolkata number. She had called it five times by the time she reached home but no luck. She didn't have much option but to wait and watch.

Rivanah was relieved to be home at last and have mom-made food. Mumbai for her was a battlefield where there was no time to rest, to be oneself and, most important, to live life the way one wanted to. Her father impressed her by gifting her a sketch stand. She had only mentioned in passing that she had started to sketch again.

'I haven't given you anything from a long time,' her father said. She hugged him, realizing how much she missed being pampered by her parents. It all seemed like a fairy tale now.

After the best dinner she had eaten in a long time, her mother joined her in her bedroom while she was sketching.

'I told your father that Danny has been signed for a film. He seemed to welcome the idea.'

'That's good, Mumma, but I'm in no mood to get married now.'

'Don't tell me you and Danny have broken up!' Her mother sounded scandalized.

Rivanah stopped sketching and looked at her lovingly. 'No, Mumma. Nothing like that. We both are still getting to know each other.'

'I think I will never understand this getting-to-know-each-other thing that you keep talking about. What is there to know so much?'

'You won't get it, Mumma.'

'Yes, I won't and I don't want to. Thank God I am not your age now. So confusing you youngsters are. Now sleep early. Don't stress yourself,' her mother said and left her alone. Her phone beeped with a message. It was Ekansh.

I'm going to meet Tista tomorrow in the hospital. Would you like to join me?

Of course, she replied.

Next day Ekansh met her below the Ultadanga footbridge and together they drove to the hospital on EM Bypass. The visiting hours had just started when they reached. They arrived at Tista's cabin only to find her family present there. On the bed was Tista, looking pale and weak. She tried to smile but it was clear she was very unwell. Ekansh greeted everyone and went to stand beside Tista. Rivanah introduced herself to Tista's family and stood by her bed on the other side. Tista raised her hand on seeing Rivanah who grasped it warmly.

'I can't live alone in that Mumbai flat. I want you back soon,' Rivanah said, trying to boost her morale.

'I . . . too . . . want . . . that,' Tista stuttered. Rivanah smiled at her, caressing her forehead, as Tista's father asked her not to talk much.

'You get well soon first, then we'll talk as much as we want to over a cup of your magic tea.' Rivanah said. Her phone beeped with a message. Rivanah excused herself as Ekansh started talking with Tista's parents.

Rivanah read the message. It was from the same unknown number that she had received the message a day ago.

Food court, City Centre 2. In 30 minutes. Your only chance to know who I am.

A chill ran through Rivanah's spine. *Will Argho actually reveal his identity?*

Rivanah spoke up, saying that she needed to go home because of some emergency. Ekansh glanced at her but she averted her eyes quickly and took her leave. Coming out of the hospital she took a cab to City Centre 2. She reached a few minutes late. She looked around trying to spot Argho when she got a message from the same number:

You are late, Mini. I don't like that. I will see you in Mani Square now. Food court. In exactly 40 mins.

Rivanah was enraged reading this. She replied to the message: *This better not be a game.*

And rushed out. She took a cab and clocked herself this time. She reached Mani Square mall's food court exactly ten minutes before time. She took a seat and waited for Argho to show up. She messaged on the number that she was there. The response which popped up infuriated Rivanah further:

You are early, Mini. I don't like this. Meet me in South City, food court, in an hour.

If Argho doesn't show up in South City mall this time, I will never ever talk to the stranger again, Rivanah promised herself and hailed a cab.

Ekansh called her in between, but she was too distracted to talk to him properly. She reached South City mall before time again but went inside only two minutes before the fixed time. This time she stepped on to the food court exactly on time. Few seconds later she got a message: *Look to your left.*

Rivanah did but couldn't spot Argho. Someone tapped on her shoulder from behind. Rivanah turned in a flash. *It can't be . . .* she thought and said, 'What the fuck are you doing here . . . Ishita?' Rivanah's eyes widened seeing her old roomie after ages now.

'I'm sorry, Rivanah. I never told you this.'

'Told me what?' Rivanah thought she was almost losing her voice.

'That I had a crush on you, Mini.'

All of the mall's cacophony around Rivanah turned into pin-drop silence.

26

'Please tell me this isn't true,' Rivanah said in a resigned manner. She had never seen Ishita look so serious before.

'But it is true, Mini. I love you,' Ishita said with no change in her expression.

Rivanah pulled up a chair and sat down on it with a thud. She hid her face with her hands. Nothing was making sense to her. She looked up and said, 'What's with Hiya . . .?' And noticed Ishita had an amused face.

'What?' Rivanah shrugged.

Ishita burst out laughing. For a moment Rivanah was clueless and then she got it. Her ex-roomie was kidding. *She was fucking kidding.*

'I will kill you, Ishita. I sure will,' Rivanah said, watching Ishita who was in splits by now. 'This isn't funny, Ishita.'

Realizing Rivanah was actually cross and extremely serious, Ishita stopped laughing.

'I am so sorry, babes. I thought I would surprise you.'

'But this is not the way.'

'Okay, I am sorry, yaar. What's the big deal? Don't tell me the stranger is still behind you,' Ishita said, and, looking at Rivanah, her jaw fell.

'Are you serious?'

Rivanah nodded.

'Then I'm seriously sorry.'

Rivanah took a few minutes to relay to Ishita what all had happened since she left for Gurgaon.

'So the stranger is still there somewhere? Unbelievable! What does he want?'

'I have no idea!'

'And that Hiya Chowdhury thing you told me about is fucking scary, dude!'

'Tell me about it.'

'What is the police saying?'

'I revoked my complaints.'

'Why?'

'Cinderella complex,' Rivanah lamented.

'What the fuck is that?'

'A psychiatrist told me that I constantly need a saviour in my life or else I'll go mad.'

'Holy mother of God! What have you landed yourself in?'

'And that is not all.'

Rivanah told her about Ekansh and the kitchen incident.

'Fuckin' shit! When I met you for the first time you were a girl who used to take permission from her boyfriend to go out and enjoy herself, and now, in a span of a year or so, you are telling me that girl has fucked her ex while he was in a relationship with someone else? I can't believe it.'

'Frankly, I wouldn't believe it either. Anyway, enough about me. What's up with you? How come you are in Kolkata?'

'Been here for a month. I changed jobs. Gurgaon is history now. I so wanted to contact you before but time just kept flying and here we are now.'

'I know. Even I wanted to buzz you but it just didn't happen.'

'I saw your Kolkata update on Facebook and thought of playing this prank. I had your number but I was sure you didn't have my new Kolkata number.'

'Wait. Let's go to my place. We can catch up there,' Rivanah said.

'Sounds great.'

The two girls took a cab and went straight to Rivanah's place where they caught up with their past, lessons and life.

'You know, men just don't excite me now. I mean, I am straight,' Ishita said, 'but the idea of being with a man is something I have grown out of. All are the same, they all stink. Mom and Dad want me to get married within the next year. It is only to avoid them that I came to Kolkata. I have relatives in Delhi but none in this part of the country.'

'Marriage is something I am confused about as well,' Rivanah said.

'Okay, Danny or Ekansh?' Ishita said. 'Just one name.'

'Danny.'

'Did you pick Danny because Ekansh anyway will be a part of you, but if you go with Ekansh you may end up forgetting Danny?'

Rivanah was amazed at how well Ishita knew her.

'Yes. But I don't think I will forget Danny.'

'You may get used to his absence.'

'Perhaps.'

'At least you have someone to live with,' Ishita said and sighed. The girls sat in silence till Rivanah's mother called out to them for lunch.

Post lunch, Rivanah had to go for the convocation ceremony. She dressed up and asked Ishita to join her.

'Are outsiders allowed?'

'Family is allowed. I will tell them you are my cousin.'

'Great. By the way, Ekansh will be there too?

'Yes, why?'

'Last time I had a talk with him, it wasn't really nice.' Ishita remembered how she had abused and pushed him in the mall after Rivanah had slapped him and left.

'Don't worry,' Rivanah said with a smile.

Rivanah's parents too accompanied her to the convocation ceremony. Ekansh was there but alone. They maintained a distance from each other, fearing someone would suspect the truth. The ceremony went on smoothly. The dean and a few other senior members of the college were dressed in black cloaks. And so were the students. One by one their names were called out and the dean gave them their degree, posed for an official college picture, after which the next name was called.

Rivanah was waiting impatiently for her turn. They were all standing in a line with a staff member coordinating their on-stage entry and exit. She looked at her parents once. The pride on their faces made everything worthwhile. She smiled at her mother who was beaming at her. She nudged her husband and together they signalled a thumbs-up sign to their daughter. Ishita, sitting beside her parents, too looked happy for her. Rivanah turned to look back. Ekansh was standing in the queue after some students. He was busy talking to another boy. She was happy she was done with I-hate-Ekansh phase and it wasn't exactly substituted by I-love-Ekansh. Which phase was it?

She couldn't define it. And she was happy that she couldn't. A definition brought with it its own set of problems. The next announcement made Rivanah turn to look at the announcer. He repeated the name: Hiya Chowdhury.

For some time nobody turned up. Rivanah glanced at Ishita who was already looking at her.

'Anyone from Hiya's family here?' the announcer asked. Someone in the crowd raised a hand. Rivanah leaned a bit to see Argho Chowdhury stand up.

'Please come here and receive the degree,' the announcer said. Dressed in casuals Argho came up to the stage, passed Rivanah, but he didn't seem to see her, or so she thought. He went, collected the degree from the dean and immediately walked out. She wanted to keep track of Argho. It could lead her to Hiya's family. Rivanah WhatsApped Ishita asking her to keep an eye on the guy who had just collected the degree on behalf of Hiya—Argho. Reading it, Ishita immediately stood up and went backstage, where Argho was.

After a couple more students, Rivanah's name was announced. She went and accepted the degree from the dean. Her father clicked a picture. She smiled, wondering if Ishita had Argho in sight or not. The moment her turn was over she rushed backstage. Neither Ishita nor Argho was there. She called the former.

'He is moving out. I'm outside your college gate.'

'Wait, I'm coming. Just keep an eye on him. It could be my only chance of finding out about Hiya.'

As Rivanah walked out, she told her parents on the phone that she would join them at home and that she was going out to celebrate with Ishita. Before they could ask where exactly they were going, Rivanah cut the line.

She joined Ishita outside the college and found her in a cab.

'Hurry up! He took a cab seconds ago.'

Rivanah climbed inside the cab and asked the driver to follow the white 'no refusal' cab ahead of it.

'How is Argho linked to Hiya?' Ishita asked. During the cab ride, Rivanah told her how she stumbled upon Argho on Facebook first, followed him and now she was working with him in the same office, which, by no stretch of imagination, could be a coincidence.

Argho's cab stopped at the Bidhan Nagar railway station. They bought tickets and followed him into a local train towards Barrackpore. They were one compartment away. And each time the train stopped, they got down and then climbed up again to make sure Argho didn't get down. Finally they saw him get down at Agarpara. He took the bridge which was rather empty for this time of the day. Once over it he took a cycle-rickshaw. They quickly got into another rickshaw with strict instructions to follow his. It took close to twenty minutes through quiet lanes before they stopped one house away from the house in front of which Argho stopped.

'Now what?' Ishita asked.

'We can't go inside now,' Rivanah said.

'But we don't even know if it is Argho's house or Hiya's!'

'Or, if Argho's and Hiya's family live together. He had written "di" on her Facebook timeline, so chances are they are siblings.'

'Hmm.'

'I will have to come here tomorrow to check,' Rivanah said conclusively.

'We!' Ishita said firmly.

Next day both the girls were back in the afternoon at the same place. They had planned a lot—how they should introduce themselves to whoever opened the door even if it was Argho. But in the end they thought it would be best to tell a partial truth. Rivanah was Hiya's batchmate and she got to know about her death during the convocation. And hence decided to visit her home.

Ishita was the one who pressed the doorbell. They exchanged nervous glances as the door was opened by a girl.

'Is this Hiya's house?' Rivanah asked.

'Mashima! Didi ke chaiche.' The girl was the housemaid, Rivanah understood. She asked the two girls to come in. A woman came out. Her hair was dishevelled, her sari had been draped around haphazardly, and she had a weird twinkle in her eyes as if she was looking for someone. Ishita and Rivanah stood close to each other. The woman scared them. A man came out quickly after her and asked the maid in a strict voice to take the woman inside. The maid used some force but eventually was able to take the woman inside.

'I'm sorry for my wife's behaviour. Who are you?' the man asked. He was wearing a simple half-sleeved shirt and trousers.

'Uncle,' Rivanah said, 'we are Hiya's friends.'

'Okay. I'm her father. But how did you find us here?'

'A friend told us,' Rivanah said. 'We didn't know she died because we were not in college at that time. Yesterday we had our convocation and got to know there about Hiya's death.'

'What happened to her, Uncle?' Ishita asked. This dialogue was part of their last night's plan to get to the real news.

The man paused before he said, 'She hanged herself.'

'We are sorry,' Rivanah said.

'But why did she hang herself?' Ishita asked.

'I don't know,' Hiya's father said and then added, 'I only know that someone was following her for some time.'

Rivanah and Ishita looked at each other with horror.

'Who?' Rivanah managed to ask.

'I don't know,' Hiya's father said and then added, 'One minute.' He went inside.

'I don't get it,' Ishita said. 'Was this the same stranger who was following Hiya? And if Argho is the stranger then was he following his own sister? Wait a second; we aren't sure they are siblings, right?'

'Right,' Rivanah said, trying to think clearly but failing miserably. Hiya's father came out and said, 'I found these in her room where she hanged herself.'

What Hiya's father held in his hand were white paper chits which had messages on them. As Ishita read those messages aloud one after the other, Rivanah hoped it was a dream, or else she wouldn't be able to take it. They were exactly the same messages the stranger had given her from the moment she climbed into the Meru cab on her first day in Mumbai.

'But weren't these sent to . . .' Ishita said and stopped. Rivanah had already realized the obvious. Hiya was stalked by the stranger, and she too had received the same messages. And then she hanged herself. Where was this stranger leading her? Was Hiya's death even a suicide or did he kill her?

'What happened?' Hiya's father asked. Neither was able to respond. Rivanah's phone buzzed with a message. It read: *I'll soon free you, Mini.*

27

Rivanah and Ishita took leave from Hiya's house. They were supposed to go back to Rivanah's house, but Rivanah's head started reeling, and she collapsed on the road, muttering, 'The stranger will kill me too.' Ishita took her to her PG lest Rivanah's parents become worried and ask all sorts of questions. After resting in Ishita's PG for a while, Rivanah finally felt somewhat normal.

'This is far more serious and sinister than we ever thought, Rivanah,' Ishita said. The two were alone in the PG at the time.

"I'm sure the stranger killed Hiya and made it look like a suicide. And perhaps he wants me to take the blame for it; otherwise he would have killed me too.'

'But why you? If it was only about taking blame then it could have been anybody,' Ishita argued. 'Try to connect to him and ask him for a talk,' she suggested. Rivanah sent a message to the numbers she had of the stranger. None of the messages were delivered.

'Damn, we forgot to even ask if Argho was Hiya's brother,' Ishita said.

'How does it matter now? I'm in the line of fire. I will soon be dead like Hiya.'

'Shut up, Rivanah. You have to be strong. If the stranger gets even a hint of your weakness he will not spare you.'

'He won't spare me anyway.'

'The only way ahead is cracking this whole puzzle,' Ishita said and heard Rivanah's phone ringing. It was her mother.

'Pick up the call and don't sound grim,' Ishita said, giving the phone to Rivanah. She took it after a moment's hesitation.

'Hello, Mumma.'

'Mini, when are you two coming home? Should I prepare lunch or you both are eating out?' her mother asked.

'Mumma, we will eat out and also I will come home tomorrow as I am at Ishita's place.'

'In Kolkata itself, right?'

'Yes, in Kolkata itself. You don't worry. Let Baba know. I shall be home tomorrow morning.'

'Okay Mini, take care. I will call at night.' Her mother put the phone down and continued to clean her daughter's room. She arranged the bed, the bookshelf and finally moved the sketch board to a corner in order to make space in the room. As Mrs Bannerjee held the sketch board her eyes fell on the last sketch. Her lips slowly parted in disbelief as she gaped at the sketch. She immediately called up her husband.

'Hello, what is it?' Mr Bannerjee asked.

I . . . I saw something.' Mrs Bannerjee sounded as if she had seen a ghost.

'What is it? Tell me quickly. I'm in a meeting.'

'Mini has sketched . . .'

'So?'

'Mini has sketched Hiya Chowdhury's face.'

There was a pause.

'I'm coming home now,' Mr Bannerjee said and added, 'Just keep it away from Mini.' The line went dead. Mrs Bannerjee's hands were still trembling but she somehow managed to get the paper off the sketch board.

At Ishita's PG, they were still discussing Hiya.

'And you know the worst part?' Rivanah said. 'I don't even remember Hiya. Like, I don't know how she looks.'

'What are you saying?'

'That's true.'

Rivanah's phone buzzed with a message. It was from one of the stranger's numbers. It read: *Know Your Worth, Mini. For all your answers lie within you.*

To be continued . . .

Acknowledgements

A huge thank you to Gurveen, Shruti and each and every one at Penguin Random House for bringing out this book and my previous ones just the way they should be.

When you have very few close friends you don't really have to name them: they know it without being mentioned. Thank you for being there. Sometimes that's all that matters.

Thanks to each one of my readers who has overwhelmed me with appreciation mails and messages for Book One of the Stranger trilogy and has kept me on my toes to make sure Book Two is equally good. I hope you love it as much as you loved Book One.

Special thanks to all those 'strangers' I come across every day on the road—at traffic signals, in trains, flights and where-not—whose names I don't know, and yet they help me knit stories.

Last but not the least, love and gratitude for my family for standing by me and my decisions.

About the Author

Novoneel Chakraborty is the author of five bestselling romantic thriller novels. He works in Indian television and films and lives in Mumbai. You can reach him at:
www.facebook.com/officialnbc
Email: novosphere@gmail.com
Twitter: @novoxeno
Instagram: @novoneelchakraborty

Book 3 in the Stranger Trilogy . . .

When Rivanah finds out that Hiya too had received the same messages she did, she freaks out. More so because Hiya was found hanging in her room, and Rivanah has good reason to believe it wasn't a suicide after all. Maybe Hiya was murdered in cold blood . . . and maybe she is the stranger's next victim.

But why would the stranger intend to kill Rivanah? Is Argho the stranger? Will Rivanah be able to find her link to Hiya, whose face she says she doesn't remember but is able to sketch? And if this was not enough of a mess already, Rivanah will have to choose between her first love, Ekansh, and true love, Danny, as well. Whom will she choose?

As the stranger closes in on Rivanah, leaving her with no options but to piece this elaborate puzzle together, the series finale races towards a heartbreaking finish . . .

Book 3 in the Stranger trilogy out in the winter of 2015!